C0-AWP-628

THEATRE-IN-THE-ROUND

MARGO JONES

Theatre-in-the-Round

Rinehart & Company, Inc.

New York and Toronto

Chapter Six, "The Future: A Dream and a Plan,"
appeared in the Spring, 1951, issue
of the *Southwest Review.*

TO MY MOTHER AND FATHER

I wish to express my deep gratitude
to Theodore Apstein
for his valuable help and co-operation
in preparing this book.

M. J.

CONTENTS

The above illustrations will be found between pages 148 and 149.

THEATRE-IN-THE-ROUND

CHAPTER ONE

Theatre-in-the-Round Then and Now

The dream of all serious theatre people in the United States in the middle of our twentieth century is the establishment of a national theatre, in which playwrights, actors, directors, designers, technicians and business managers can find an expression for their art and craft as well as earn a livelihood, and which will provide audiences with beautiful plays. If this dream has not yet become a reality, it is mainly because of the economic problems involved, but a solution is imperative lest all the wonderful ideals remain in a misty realm. Dreaming is a great human experience, but unless you can make your dreams come true, you cannot be of much help in creating a great theatre in America. Dreams and ideals must be combined with practical thought and action, and I firmly believe that this can be done in the theatre. If you add achievement to idealism, you prove that it is not only spiritually compensating to be idealistic, but it is also smart and profitable.

We must create the theatre of tomorrow today. We

cannot postpone our dreams and ideals any longer. Our potential audiences all over America are waiting for the theatre we have been promising them. They are eager and ready to see good plays well produced, and we must not disappoint them. Let us stir up the practical realization of a potential, of a dream, of an ideal!

What our country needs today, theatrically speaking, is a resident professional theatre in every city with a population of over one hundred thousand. According to the 1940 census figures, there are over one hundred such cities in the United States. For reasons which will become evident in this book, I believe it would be easier to start in the larger centers, although I am certain that once all these cities acquired resident professional theatres, smaller communities would want them, too; and possibly within some ten years the one hundred and seven cities whose population runs from fifty to one hundred thousand would also have their own theatres.

I have heard that there is the fantastic number of five hundred thousand groups which produce plays in this country. If this figure is even remotely accurate, it is both amazing and sufficient; but it does not tell us anything about the quality of their productions. I believe that the best way to assure quality is to give birth to a movement which will establish permanent resident professional theatres throughout the country.

I realize that this is not a new dream, but today it

does not have to be merely a dream because there is a way to do it. One of the problems that have confronted promoters and directors who have sought to establish professional theatres previously has been the building situation. Theatre construction in the United States is at a standstill, except for a few universities that have acquired handsome theatres in recent years. Former legitimate houses have either become moving-picture theatres or have been condemned or torn down. To build new theatres in desirable locations is a tremendously expensive, if not completely prohibitive, proposition if the investment has to be repaid, because the profits simply are not large enough.

The answer which I have found in Dallas and which many theatre people are finding today lies in theatre-in-the-round presentations. This form is also known as central staging, arena staging, circus theatre and penthouse style. It means very simply that you dispense with the proscenium stage and place your actors in a lighted area, surrounding them on all four sides by the spectators.

Since this method has been rediscovered and since we know that it works, there is an urgency about starting theatres in every town in the United States as soon as possible and doing it in the best way. I want to show in this book not only that it can be done, but that it must be done right or it is not worth doing. A new medium can be a challenge and a source of great theatrical excitement, provided it is not cheapened or exploited to do the same old things in the same old ways. It is the duty of everyone who works in the theatre or intends to work in it and who loves it to keep it alive, to bring more audiences into it and to improve it every minute, every month, every year.

Numerous groups have discovered that they can solve their housing problems by using theatre-in-the-round. The vast majority of these has been nonprofessional; several, however, are of professional caliber—Theatre '50, the Penthouse Theatre of Atlanta, the Arena of New York, the Music Circus at Lambertville, New Jersey, and a few others. Here is a proven way for the immediate establishment of resident professional theatres. The only way we can have a true theatrical renaissance in America is to have resident professional theatres in all our large cities. I say these theatres must be resident because they should give the community as well as the staff an assurance of continuity, and they must be professional because, if we insist on the highest standards of production, the actors and staff must spend eight hours a day in the theatre. If we want young people of talent and intelligence to go into this field and give the best they have, we must offer them the compensation of dignity and security.

Every town in America wants theatre! It is the duty and business of a capable theatre person to go into the communities of this country and create fine theatres. It takes time and courage and patience. Anyone who undertakes such an assignment must want to do it and want to do it terribly. If no substitute will be good enough, if no compromise is effected, if standards are not lowered, the objective will be accomplished. It is a matter of hard work, positive thinking, endurance and, above all, great faith. Theatre '50 in Dallas is not a phenomenon. It can be done everywhere. If cities are ready for enlarged industry, for modern hotels, for fine shops, they are also ready for good theatre.

My seeming insistence on theatre-in-the-round as a method is not fanatical. As I will point out later, I believe that ideally we should have flexible theatres, and I have as much love and admiration for the proscenium stage as for the open-air theatre or theatre-in-the-round. It would be absurd to say "we have found a practical way to create theatres, so let us do away with all other types." Not at all. I think we should have all sorts of theatre structures, and all new architectural developments should be followed and studied and utilized whenever the opportunity presents itself. But we have an urgent job ahead of us in the theatre, and a way to do it without further delay is theatre-in-the-round.

There is no doubt that a change has been occurring in the state of our theatre. The diminishing number of Broadway playhouses is terrifying at first glance, but rather than a sign of death I interpret it as a sign of change. A theatre is not decaying if, within five short years, it presents to the public two great playwriting talents like

Tennessee Williams and Arthur Miller—to mention only the most outstanding—and new actors, directors, designers and musicians. Perhaps because of the severe financial demands on a Broadway production, the standards are very high. A certain unevenness is inevitable in any theatre, but basically I believe Broadway is at a height of development in its standards of play selection and production. Too little has been said in favor of the Broadway scene. At the moment it still stands as the center of our theatre, contains its best plays, the best actors and the best stage sets and lighting to be found in America. And it is also an experimental theatre in the sense that it will risk its all on new plays and unknown playwrights. For this alone Broadway deserves the respect and admiration of every theatre person in the country.

This theatrical center of ours, nevertheless, is frighteningly small. There are only twenty-eight legitimate playhouses in the Broadway area today, and rumors are persistent about one which is to be torn down and another which is to be taken over by a television studio. Whatever the reasons may be—and the real estate situation in the New York theatre is extremely difficult—it means that the center of our activities is narrowing down. It does not mean that the American theatre is dying, for, even in New York there are areas besides Broadway where the theatre can flourish, and we have hundreds of cities where potential audiences are starved for good theatre.

The fact that last season there were only sixty productions on Broadway, while twenty-five years ago there were over two hundred, is an unmistakable sign of change, as is the decreasing number of plays that go out on the road. In the late 'twenties, some hysterical notes were sounded because only seventy road companies were entertaining the nation, but in the 1949-50 season there were only thirty-two! Nor is the outlook good for the 1950-51 season.

In connection with the "road," we might also examine the value it has for the theatregoer. If it were financially possible for the best plays from New York to be toured without lowering the quality of the production, they would undoubtedly provide audiences with superb entertainment. The trouble is that because of the incredibly high cost of touring, it is often out of the question to maintain desired standards on the road. An even more serious handicap of the "road" is the lack of continuity. The audience can never be sure of getting plays throughout the season, and short stands in each city are no substitute for a resident professional theatre which can provide its audience with a play every night.

Some special touring companies, differing from the regular "road" in that they are not former Broadway productions (notably Margaret Webster's Shakespearean troupe), are doing a great deal to whet the appetite of theatregoers in America. They are few and far between and, again, do not offer any continuity to the audience.

Summer stock, which decreased tremendously during the war years, is very much alive now, but it still remains concentrated in the Northeast, although summer theatres are springing up in other parts of the country, too. Of course this type of theatre is a godsend to the actor from an economic point of view as well as a way to gain experience, but the short rehearsal period (one week usually) and the star system (which frequently means that the star only has two or three rehearsals with the rest of the company) are unsatisfactory in the long run. Another shortcoming of the summer theatre is its brief season, during which new plays are seldom offered (a notable exception is the Westport Country Playhouse).

The community theatre movement, ever since the days of the Provincetown, has contributed considerably in bringing theatre to the people of this country. In addition to entertaining its audiences, the community theatre has frequently proved to be an excellent training ground for actors. But since community theatres have not been able to offer financial security to most of their workers, too few of them have found it possible to devote the necessary time to find and produce new plays; those which have assumed this responsibility in spite of great difficulties have been of invaluable aid to the American playwright.

Another type of nonprofessional theatre which has appeared recently is the "off-Broadway" group. It consists of young actors and directors who produce plays in noncommercial playhouses, mostly to exhibit their talents to the professional theatre. The majority of these groups has sprung up in New York and in the Los Angeles-Hollywood area. They are magnificent training centers for actors, directors, designers and for playwrights (if, of course, they do new plays, which too few of them do), but their efforts have been too sporadic to provide a consistent theatre to any kind of audience. I believe these groups could have more continuity in the theatre if they realized that their main aim is still to produce a good play in the best possible manner and not to be a showcase for actors and directors. If their productions are good, they will automatically function as showcases, but they will also be improving the standards of the American theatre, which some of them undoubtedly have been doing by presenting new plays and new talent.

There has been notable progress in the educational theatre. Every year more colleges and universities are establishing drama departments, and those which already have them are adding new courses to their curriculums and enriching their staffs with professional theatre people. This is of vast importance because most of our young theatre people will emerge from this kind of theatre. Since its main duty is the preparation and training of actors, technicians, playwrights and directors, the university theatre must approach professional standards as much as possible, both by having instructors with professional experience and by assuming a sound theatre attitude in its productions.

I hope that this much-too-brief summary of theatrical activity in the United States shows an encouraging picture. If I have stopped to point out the flaws and drawbacks in each type of theatre, it is only because I feel so strongly that we must improve in every branch of the field and that we must have first-rate theatres at every level. It gives me a deep satisfaction to hear that a new theatre is being born anywhere, for I always trust that it will be a fine theatre. I see no reason for starting one that will not be fine. Much as I would like to see theatre flourishing across America, I want to state very firmly that I believe bad theatre is worse than no theatre at all.

In passing I have mentioned the status of the actor in connection with these different theatres. Actors, like all people, need security. In September of 1949, Actors' Equity Association reported a total membership of 6,408, while the median figure of employment for the year was 1,115; that is only 19%. Maximum theatrical unemployment in 1949 was 86.4% and minimum 70.3%. One out of two actors who performed in the year of this survey had gross earnings up to $760. The lowest one fourth made $305 or less. One in four made $2,540 or more. Half of those working earned between $305 and $2,540. The survey, prepared by Alan Hewitt, states: "Actors have greater expenses than the average worker; these include clothes, make-up, agents' commissions, telephone services and the like. In this era of high prices for food and rent, a frugal subsistence living for an unmarried actor would be $55 a week in take-home pay, figured as a gross annual income of $3,500 before deductions. Fewer than one in five (857—18.3%) made that amount from work in the theatre." The median income, Mr. Hewitt reports, was $465.

Without going into more detailed statistics, it is obvious that we must offer our actors a better livelihood if they are to remain in the theatre or if we are to attract highly talented people into this medium. The answer is simple—we must have resident professional theatres in every city of more than one hundred thousand population in the United States.

Talented young people come to New York and find themselves in a bottleneck. They are discouraged, though many of them remain in New York, working towards a mythical glamour and the large earnings which not even 5% of Equity's membership attain. If these young people could return to their home towns or go to other cities and work in professional theatres, their ambitions would be achieved someday.

The glamour of the theatre lies in working in the theatre, no matter where it may be. There is no doubt that the actor gets a certain stimulation from being with other people in his field who are intensely interested in everything that is happening around them; the air they breathe seems to be charged with theatrical excitement. At the moment the actor is not likely to find such an atmosphere outside of New York City unless he goes out and creates it—and this can be done.

And what wonderful training he will get! He will be able to perform a variety of roles during one season, and some of them will be parts which he might not have played on Broadway until he had been "around" for ten or fifteen years. Good actors are made by the variety of parts they play. It is interesting to notice that almost every actor or actress of any stature who has come to this country from England was at one time or another connected with the Old Vic repertory.

There is no problem in obtaining good actors for resident professional theatres outside of New York City. Nothing tempts an actor more than a guarantee of thirty or forty (and perhaps eventually fifty-two) weeks of assured work and salary in a professional theatre doing a large number of new scripts. It is true that radio and television assignments help many New York actors to make ends meet, but potential jobs in these fields are open all over America.

People are wondering why we do not have any young stars in the theatre. Our established stars have been famous for twenty years. Where are the new ones? Most of our established stars got their training in the old stock companies. Today, when the stock company no longer exists, a young actor struggles to get work on Broadway. If he is lucky enough to land a part and the play is successful, he will have an income for a while and he will develop his art, but not nearly as much as if he were playing a variety of roles during a season. In this connection, an organization like the Actors' Studio—where a select group of professional actors can do exercises and scenes and develop further in their work—is wonderful.

The case of the director, the designer and the technician is similar. There have not been enough available jobs for them in the theatre because there has not been sufficient professionalization. Their solution, too, lies in the resident professional theatre.

The playwright's situation is somewhat though not altogether different. The opportunities for the playwright have narrowed down so much, and there is so little activity in the production of new manuscripts, that the talented writer with inclinations towards the stage tends to go into other fields. The question of what comes first, the theatre or the play, is like the chicken-or-the-egg question. I say the play comes first. Of course you must have a theatre, but you must have a play—or a group of plays—which you are anxious to put on. The desire to do a play is the greatest incentive to starting a theatre. We can make the next decade a golden era of American drama, but first we must have great playwrights, and the way to find them and develop them is to produce new plays. Some of them will be fine, others not so fine, and still others quite bad, but among their authors we will uncover the true playwriting talents and we will foster their improvement. I believe that there are unheralded authors throughout this country writing plays which cry out for production, and I also believe that there are fine writers in other fields who would turn to playwriting if they knew that there was a chance to get a first-rate production for their manuscripts with enough compensation. There is a chance now, but it is slim, and it is both heartening and surprising that so many writers devote their time and souls and energy to dramaturgy and that so many younger people are enrolling in playwriting courses every semester in numberless schools. Productions by resident professional theatres all over the country could provide the playwright with a considerable income. There is no reason why a number of resident theatres could not produce a worthy new play simultaneously. Of course I am assuming that the productions would be of high quality, comparable to a first-class production on Broadway. It is also conceivable—and very advisable, the moment the budget permits it—that each theatre will have a resident playwright who will be on the staff and thus will be provided with security as well as an opportunity to see his play on its feet.

The American theatre has developed a new form—the musical play—which has become very popular with audiences in New York and throughout the country. When St. John Terrell opened the Music Circus at Lambertville, he made it possible to present the musical play without the tremendous expense involved in the production of a Broadway musical. With the spread of the music circuses to Hyannis and Danbury in the summer and to Miami in the winter (with many others already being planned), vast new audiences are being found for this form. It is a young form and, like other types of theatre, it needs new talent. There are many young composers and writers in America working on musical plays and they find it difficult to be produced on Broadway because of the financial output required. The music circuses could be the ideal center for the first productions of new musical plays; in other words they could do for the composer, the lyricist and the librettist what the other resident professional theatres can do for the playwright.

What I have said about the functions of the different theatres and about the situation of theatre people in America points in the direction of decentralization, a word that has been used in the theatre a great deal for a number of years. The community and college theatres have contributed considerably to this decentralization, but the professional theatre continues to have its mainstay in New York, with a few exceptions like the Barter Theatre, the Artillery Lane Playhouse, Theatre '50 and a few others which do not operate the whole year round.

Three organizations on a national level have labored hard and are continuing their work to decentralize the

American theatre. These are the American National Theatre and Academy (ANTA), the National Theatre Conference (NTC), and the American Educational Theatre Association (AETA). This summary of the state of our theatre would be incomplete without a brief discussion of each one of these.

The American National Theatre and Academy was chartered on July 5, 1935, by the Congress of the United States of America, and its preamble reads: "A people's project, organized and conducted in their interest, free from commercialism, but with the firm intent of being as far as possible self-supporting. A national theatre should bring to the people throughout the country their heritage of the great drama of the past and the best of the present, which has been too frequently unavailable to them under existing conditions." Only a few other organizations—like the American Red Cross and the Smithsonian Institution—have been granted such charters.

Senate Bill 2642, which established ANTA as a nonprofit corporation, outlined its purposes:

A. The presentation of theatrical productions of the highest type.

B. The stimulation of public interest in the Drama as an art belonging to the Theatre and to Literature and therefore to be enjoyed both on the stage and in the study.

C. The advancement of interest in drama through the United States of America by furthering production of plays of the highest type, interpreted by the best actors at a minimum cost.

D. The further development of the study of the drama of the present and past in our universities, colleges, schools and elsewhere.

E. The sponsoring, encouraging and development of the art and technique of the theatre through a school within the American National Theatre and Academy.

The Charter, it should be noted, did not carry a federal grant, and the founders, who were not theatre people, waited for a plan of action before making any attempt to raise funds for the organization. The fact that such a plan was not immediately forthcoming is not to be attributed to the negligence of theatre people, for in 1935 Federal Theatre was established, and it was expected to fill the need for a national theatre in America. When Congress dissolved Federal Theatre in 1939, the Executive Committee of ANTA invited Robert Sherwood to become president and set up a board of directors to be chosen mostly from theatre leaders. This task was interrupted by the war, and the organization was virtually nonexistent until October of 1945, when Robert Breen and Robert Porterfield submitted a plan for a National Theatre Foundation (not unlike the Arts Council of Great Britain). The Board accepted the idea in principle, and in 1946 ANTA became a working institution with the appointment of Robert Breen as Executive Secretary.

ANTA now has representative membership in every state of the Union, and its main purpose is "to extend the living theatre beyond present limitations by bringing the best in the theatre to every state in the Union."

ANTA is the central clearing house of all types of theatre, and it established a long-needed bond between the professional and nonprofessional theatres. ANTA's activities since 1946 are so various and widespread that they are difficult to summarize and omissions are inevitable. Its countless services include: the answering of technical questions and business and promotion problems; placement of directors, technicians, business managers and teachers; arranging appearances of guest artists; providing expert advice on starting new companies at all levels; maintaining a speakers' and conference bureau throughout the country; preparing a monthly department for *Theatre Arts Magazine,* headed "Theatre: USA" and putting out a news letter for its membership; acting as the American headquarters of the International Theatre Institute and as a center to which foreign theatre people can come for information about any phase of the American theatre (this phase of ANTA's work has been under the magnificent leadership of Rosamond Gilder); running an Experimental Theatre and an Invitational Series for two seasons in New York City for the production of unusual and worthy manuscripts; maintaining a script department which has fostered seventy-two productions of new plays and has given thirty-nine playwrights an opportunity to see their plays in performance; sponsoring a series of radio and television broadcasts; recording an album of scenes from great plays interpreted by outstanding actors; presenting the yearly "ANTA Album," which consists of scenes and moments from exciting productions of the past enacted, whenever possible, by their original casts; and in spite of its own limited funds, ANTA has made gifts and loans to several worth-while ventures.

Only recently ANTA has acquired the Guild Theatre in New York, which had been a radio house for several years, and considerable energy has been expended to operate a theatre in Washington, D. C. There is no doubt that ANTA is working hard towards the establishment of a national theatre, and in the creation and continuance of resident professional theatres ANTA has been and will be of invaluable aid and service.

The National Theatre Conference is a co-operative organization of directors of community and university theatres organized collectively to serve the noncommercial theatre. The current activities of the Conference include the publication of a Bulletin; the operation of a placement service; the securing of new plays written by established playwrights especially for the noncommercial theatre or released to community and university theatres prior to a New York opening; the sponsorship of a New York Tryout Studio to assist young actors to find employment; the awarding of fellowships to playwrights, directors and other potential leaders; and the encouragement of regional theatre workers through support of Regional Drama Conferences. During World War II, the National Theatre Conference initiated the program that later was taken over by the War Department under the name of Soldier Shows. These projects have been administered for the benefit of all noncommercial theatres. The aim of the Conference is the stimulation of interest in the theatre as a vital contribution to our national life, and the training and encouragement of leaders who will create and strengthen professional noncommercial theatres that enrich the communities they serve and constitute in their totality a truly National Theatre.

The American Educational Theatre Association is an organization devoted to raising the standards and improving the quality of theatrical activities in this country at all levels from the children's theatre, through the secondary school, to the college and university. AETA's work also affects the community theatre, the adult-education programs and various regional groups. All of AETA's members have a voice in the administration of the organization through their representatives in the Advisory Council and on the Executive Board. In 1949, the Association launched a quarterly *Educational Theatre Journal*, devoted to the publication of research reports, bibliographies and projects of interest to people in the educational theatre field. AETA also sponsors an annual Children's Theatre Conference.

I believe that the aims and activities of these organizations show not only the tendency of the American theatre to decentralize, but also the increasing interest on the part of professional theatre people to help in the establishment of units outside of Broadway.

Decentralization is good, but there is something else we need if we are to have a great theatre in America, and that is a sound theatre attitude. It is high time all of us who work in the theatre—whether it is Broadway, resident professional, community, college or high school—adopted an attitude with the finest possible standards.

All types of theatre are really *one*, because if theatre is to be exciting its aim is always *one*: to present good plays in the best possible manner. What is most important in maintaining a sound theatre attitude is the reason for choosing and producing a play; this reason should be that it is a fine play, you are excited by it and you can give it a good production. When a college director, for instance, chooses to do *The Taming of the Shrew* for this reason, he has a sound theatre attitude. An automatic by-product will be the training his students will receive from acting in this play, working on the production and observing it. Thus, as a result of his sound theatre attitude, the director will also perform his duty as an educator.

A sound theatre attitude implies a great want to do a play. If a director does not have a suitable cast for that particular script, sometimes his great desire to see the play on the stage, his enthusiasm and the quality of the play itself can pull the actors up.

True excitement in the theatre stems from hard work. Anyone who decides to produce a play or to participate in its production must take his job seriously; working towards a goal of excellence will enable him to enjoy his work to the fullest extent and give him the enthusiasm which is essential in the theatre.

There is one more element in having a sound theatre attitude which I want to emphasize: the attitude towards the new playwright. The decision to do a new script is mutually beneficent for the theatre and the dramatist; the writer is fortunate to have his play produced and the group to have found a worthy play to do. The author must be paid a royalty, and his script must be given the benefit of the finest production the theatre is capable of offering.

I believe it is imperative in creating new resident professional companies to take a violent stand about the choice of plays. Personally I believe in the production of classics and new scripts, with emphasis on new scripts.

Our theatre can never be stronger than the quality of its plays. We must, therefore, have a great number of good plays. The classics have proved their value throughout the history of the theatre, and I believe we should draw on them as great literature and great theatre. But if we produce only classics, we are in no way reflecting our own age. Our theatres must not only be professional, they must be contemporary as well. The most excellent seasons in New York are those which bring forth exciting new play-writing talent.

Too many people are saying, "I'll do a new play if I can find a good one." Certainly you must find a good one, but this attitude is not good enough. The plays can be found if you look hard enough. And if you take the violent stand I have spoken about, you will feel obligated to search and search and search until the scripts are discovered. I have a belief that there is great writing in America today and that much of it has not yet been unearthed.

Great theatres have always had their playwrights. Shakespeare, Lope de Vega, Molière, Ibsen—all these were men around whom theatrical companies were functioning. The Moscow Art Theatre had Chekhov; the Abbey Theatre had Yeats, Synge and O'Casey; the Provincetown had O'Neill; the Group had Odets. We must have our new playwrights, and we will not have them unless we give them many outlets to see their plays produced. This is the best way in which they can learn to write better plays.

The production of classics is healthy, but it is not a step in the flowering we want to see in the American theatre. We need progress, and the seed of progress in the theatre lies in the new plays.

On Broadway it is not considered unusual or idealistic to do a new play. Why do theatres in other cities feel that it is? Enough of them have been very successful with the few original plays they have produced, yet they continue their policy of imitation. The Broadway producer has at least one quality which theatrical leaders elsewhere would do well to emulate—he has the courage to do new scripts.

A sound theatre attitude in reading a new script is very simple indeed. It means you pick it up and read it. If your experience and taste and discretion tell you that it is a good play, that you like it, then it *is* a good play until such a time as presented to an audience which rejects it. This can happen, of course, if the play has no meaning for the audience; but if it had a meaning for the producer or director when he read it, he should have been able to impart this meaning to the audience. The failure of a play before the public is as often the fault of the production as of the script. The producer must, however, be prepared for a complete rejection or for a mixed reaction. After all, do all people like the same type of houses, clothes, furniture, paintings? Then, why must they all like the same play? Five New York producers discussing a play will disagree violently on its merits, but one of them believes in it, puts it on and may have a success on his hands.

Looking for a play is a great adventure. I know of no greater satisfaction than to pick up a script and find that it is good, that it has never been done before and that the opportunity is yours to present it before an audience. I consider myself exceptionally lucky because once I have found the script, I have the means to produce it. I feel the same thing should be happening to many people all over this great nation.

Today we have the possibility of starting a great theatre movement in America. It must be done well or it is not worth doing. It must be done in terms of resident professional theatres producing new plays and classics. And because of the special economic situation in which the theatre finds itself at present, it seems the most practical way is to do it in theatre-in-the-round.

A few words should be said about the historical background of this technique, for, although it is only now begininning to spread throughout America, it is not new at all, but perhaps the oldest form of theatre known to the human race.

Robert Edmond Jones once gave a hypothetical account of the first drama, born when the leader of the tribe told his people how he killed the lion and told it in terms of action. Before he started his story, he said to his tribe: "Sit around me in a circle—you and you and you—right here, where I can reach out and touch you all." This implies both intimacy and central staging, which are the two main attributes of theatre-in-the-round today.

Drama began with storytelling and tribal dances, and it is natural to assume that the audience surrounded the tellers or the performers, for when something occurs on the street, when there is a fight or an argument, observers always surround the contendents.

Some four thousand years ago the Passion Play of Osiris was performed in Egypt. Celebrating the death of Osiris, it was a procession from the palace to the temple and took place on a float which represented the sacred boat of Osiris. Presumably spectators did not sit in front of this float but stood or walked around it or at least on three sides of it. If these are assumptions, we do have facts about the beginnings of the Greek theatre.

Both tragedy and comedy had as their source the songs to the god Dionysus known as dithyrambs, and these were first chanted in processions with the people standing around those who sang and danced. As the structure of the Greek theatre developed, the main acting area (or rather dancing area) was the orchestra, and in years to follow it continued to be the circular dancing space for the chorus. Originally the altar (thymele) was located in the center of the orchestra, and the statue of Dionysus was placed near the altar. Undoubtedly when these performances first began, the audience surrounded the dancers; but as the decision was made to seat the audience on a hillside, the amphitheatre structure appeared, and since a hillside slopes in one direction only, the circle was cut to little more than a semicircle. The circular space for the action of the chorus continued to be there, however, and the *skene* (which eventually developed into our stage) was nothing but a retiring room in which the actor could change his mask or costume. All the acting was done on the ground level—that is in the orchestra. Virtually no scenery was employed in the Greek theatre; that is, the dramatists relied on the imagination of the audience, but the costuming was very elaborate.

The Graeco-Roman theatres also stretched beyond the semicircle, but the orchestra was reduced from its full circle and the scenic façade became quite elaborate. This was carried even further in the Roman buildings which were on level ground and became exact semicircles, giving the same shape to the orchestra, which was now used as seating space for the audience on certain occasions. Still, Rome did not do away with the "arena style" completely. The ferocious spectacles which Roman audiences really preferred to the theatre were staged in the Colosseum and the Circus Maximus, and auditoria bowls with lake centers (*naumachiae*) were built to stage sea fights.

After the decline of Rome, portion of plays were performed by traveling actors on streets or at court festivities. These shows, which filled the theatrical horizon from the sixth to the twelfth century, were mostly one-man shows played to an intimate audience which stood or sat on at least three sides of them.

With the rise of the liturgical drama in the medieval church, again a natural setting was provided for a play. The different portions of the church were used as sets, and the audience was conveniently distributed in the church, the degree of intimacy depending on the size of the temple. As the demand for these plays became greater, they were moved to the steps of the church, and it is logical to suppose that the audience stood in a semicircle (or more) to watch them.

The mystery and miracle cycles, played on wagon stages in different parts of a town, were seen by an audience on three sides of them.

The Italian Renaissance brought the development of painted scenery and, with the desire to gain perspective in the painting, the proscenium frame came into being. It did not replace the other type of theatre for a long time, however since the first theatres to be built with a proscenium still had a ballroom floor on which pageants could be staged. Masques, too, continued to be played in "ballroom theatres," in which the action took place both on the stage and in the center of the room (an example of flexible staging). In many banquet halls, square stages were erected in the center for dancing and plays.

The improvised comedy of the Renaissance, the popular *commedia dell' arte,* which was to inspire so many of the great writers of comedy, started its long life in the theatre on small platforms located in public squares, with a democratic audience watching on all three sides. Virtually no sets were employed at first, and all the lavishness came from the substantial acting.

The short religious and secular plays in Spain, which preceded the Golden Age of Lope de Vega and Tirso de Molina and Calderón de la Barca, were performed on platform stages in courtyards (*corrales*). The Golden Age theatre, very similar to the Elizabethan stages, had spectators on three sides.

Before the period known as the Elizabethan in the English theatre, plays were presented in halls, banquet chambers, inn yards and on the village green. Most satisfactory of all these places was the inn yard because of its shape and structure. It is not surprising, therefore, that the Elizabethan theatre evolved from the inn into a circular or polygonal shape. The typical Elizabethan theatre had three tiers of galleries roofed over with thatch or tile while the center remained open. The platform stage projected halfway into the pit, and the spectators sat on three sides of the stage. At the rear of the platform there was an alcove or inner stage, separated by a draw-curtain and flanked by doors. Over the alcove stage was an upper stage also with a curtain, but in front of this curtain a balcony projected slightly over the platform. Occasionally this balcony was used to seat spectators who were more concerned with being seen than with seeing the play. A few spectators were also allowed to sit on the stage from time to time.

Little or no scenery was used in the Elizabethan theatre, but elaborate props and extravagant costumes made up for the lack of scenery. Gorgeous colors and fantastic cuts were to be found in the costuming, and it is characteristic to observe that Henslowe, who never paid more than eight pounds for a script, spent as much as twenty pounds for a cloak.

In the eighteenth century, with the development of the tennis-court theatre in France, shelf-acting became the trend. But the apron which projected into the audience was still employed in many theatres as a means of contacting the audience. It was the last link of intimacy before the theatre retired completely behind the proscenium arch and the footlights.

Similar types of theatres are to be found in China and Japan. In the Chinese theatre the stage is a platform twenty-five feet square and five or six feet high projecting into the audience (although a balustrade runs around the stage to separate it from the audience). No front curtain is used; the furniture and props, which are highly stylized, are always in view and are even changed in front of the audience. While the ground spectators sit in front of the stage, the gallery runs around three sides of the auditorium.

The Nō plays of the Japanese theatre are performed on a square projecting platform which is linked by a bridge to the greenroom, the audience sitting on three sides of the stage. Very elaborate costuming is used. The Kabuki or popular theatre of Japan originally utilized a platform in an open space; but later, under the influence of the Nō drama, it employed the bridge, and still later two long runways from the corners of the stage through the audience, with a balcony on three sides.

Although we have said that the proscenium stage appeared early in the seventeenth century and became the principal trend in the eighteenth century, it is interesting to notice that Goethe, in the 1770's, wanted a larger forestage for his theatre at Weimar in order to re-establish the direct contact between actor and audience which had existed in the Elizabethan theatre.

Undoubtedly there were times—some of them perhaps not even recorded in the history of the theatre—when directors and actors sought to return to the intimate form, but the first strong movement in that direction appeared in the first quarter of our century, especially among French and German theatre artists. Copeau, Reinhardt, Dalcroze and Appia seem to have originated the movement more or less simultaneously.

To Jacques Copeau goes the credit for opening the first presentational theatre of our times in the Western world—the Théâtre du Vieux Colombier, founded in 1913. Copeau, as Kenneth MacGowan says in his *Continental Stagecraft,* "proposed to take the hall that his resources permitted, and to make it over to suit the spirit of his company. He could build no ideal playhouse, but he could make one in which his actors could escape the realisms and pretenses of the modern theatre, and would play to and with the audience as their spirit demanded." In the Théâtre du Vieux Colombier steps led not only from the stage to the forestage, but also from the forestage to the ground level where the audience sat. There was no proscenium arch; in addition to the permanent structure a few properties and screens or curtains were used to suggest the locale and mood of the play. Footlights were dispensed with, the light emanating from four large lamps placed in the auditorium and visible to the public. A similar theatre (the Marais) was designed in Brussels under the supervision of Copeau's close collaborator, Louis Jouvet.

In Germany, Max Reinhardt, who had started his career as a director in an intimate theatre in 1902, had already staged at the Circus Schumann Sophocles' *Oedipus Rex* (1910), *Sumurûn* (1910), Hofmannsthal's version of *Everyman* and Volmoeller's adaptation of Maeterlinck's *Sister Beatrice* known as *The Miracle* (1911). The spectacle was huge, but Reinhardt was still preoccupied with the problem of maintaining intimacy. In the production of *Oedipus*—in which he used the central area of the circus as well as a stage modeled after the Greek theatre—the actors made their entrances and exits from the orchestra and the balconies, almost mingling with the audience. With *Sumurûn* he put runways over the heads of the audience, using as his inspiration the runways of the Japanese theatre. In the Circus Schumann, the audience was seated in one tier of seats arranged on three sides of the central space.

After World War I, Reinhardt remodeled the Circus Schumann into an enormous theatre, the Grosses Schauspielhaus, which was a combination of a Greek and modern theatre. After the financial failure of this venture, Reinhardt turned his attention to the Redoutensaal of Vienna, a baroque room which was designed in 1774 as the Empress Maria Theresa's ballroom. Here his stage was a roofless shell without proscenium or curtain, and most of the light came from chandeliers which also lighted the audience.

Reinhardt's circus experiments were imitated in Paris by Firmin Gémier, director of the Odéon Theatre, who opened the Cirque D'Hiver as a huge spectacle house.

Jacques Dalcroze's School of Eurhythmics in Hellerau, near Dresden, presented plays in an oblong hall, the stage being the floor of the hall itself. It was there that Dalcroze and the great Swiss designer, Adolphe Appia, joined forces to present Paul Claudel's *The Tidings Brought to Mary* on a central platform reached by stairways on either side, with smaller platforms placed upon the larger one.

Employing platforms and staircases to suggest locale and to bring the play closer to the audience was the favorite method of Leopold Jessner, director of the State Theatre of Berlin from 1919 to 1925. Jessner's settings became known as "Jessner-treppen."

The Russian theatre had also demonstarted an interest in bringing spectator and performer together. Meierhold had advanced the desire to mingle the two elements in his theatre, and Tairov was concerned with establishing intimacy in his Kamerny (chamber) Theatre. But it was left to Nikolai Okhlopkov to create a theatre devoted to this purpose. His Moscow Realistic Theatre was also the first modern theatre to use completely central staging in certain productions. Okhlopkov's theatre was flexible and different areas were utilized, but in producing Gorki's *Mother*, for instance, the stage, according to Norris Houghton's *Moscow Rehearsals*, "was a circular one set in the center of the house; then from this center there were four runways that ran along the four walls of the auditorium. Actors made all their entrances and exits to the center stage along these runways."

To clarify Okhlopkov's objectives, Houghton states: "All these devices are designed to bring about the meeting of actor and audience so that it will be impossible to separate the two—to surround the audience with actors just as the actors are surrounded by audience. In *Mother*, Okhlopkov carries this so far as to have one actor hand to any spectator sitting beside the stage a loaf and a knife for him to hold. This fusion of the two he makes much more natural than has any other director whom I have ever seen attempt the same thing. Whereas Max Reinhardt, Meierhold, and all other régisseurs have simply made the spectators more self-conscious by mingling audience and actors in ways which have seemed to destroy much illusion and theatrical unity, Okhlopkov makes the unity and the illusion stronger." Okhlopkov believed at first that this type of theatre was restricted to realism, but shortly before the closing of his theatre (1937), he began to experiment with stylized productions.

There were repercussions of these movements and experiments in the United States, chiefly through Kenneth MacGowan's two excellent books, *The Theatre of Tomorrow* and *Continental Stagecraft* (in collaboration with Robert Edmond Jones), which were published in 1921 and 1922, respectively. Besides informing the American theatre about the new type of staging that was being developed in Europe, MacGowan stimulated our imaginations with a fascinating description of a hypothetical production of *The Merchant of Venice,* done completely in arena style at the Cirque Medrano of Paris. Robert Edmond Jones supplied the description with a magnificent sketch of such a presentation.

At approximately the same time, Norman Bel Geddes, who had been experimenting with designs for new theatres for several years, came up with the plans for his now famous Theatre Number 14 for circular staging. This theatre, which was to be constructed for the Chicago World's Fair, has never been built, but it remains one of the most magnificent projects and dreams in the American theatre. I will describe it in detail in Chapter Three.

It was also in the early twenties that Hermann

Rosse, whom Sheldon Cheney considered one of the most creative talents among designers in the American theatre, proposed a circular stage to be surrounded by transparent scenery. This scenery, painted on gauze and lit from the inside, would be visible to only one portion of the audience; in other words, the spectator would see through the gauze on his side of the theatre, and the gauze on the opposite side would form a scenic background for the actors on the round stage. Rosse's design, which was prepared for a projected production of a nativity play in the Coliseum Building of Chicago, was apparently never executed; but years later Fordham University utilized a scrim in its arena theatre to separate the actors from the audience.

The first actual use of central staging in America must be credited to Azubah Latham, who directed *The Mask of Joy* at Teachers College of Columbia University in 1914, in the center of a gymnasium, with Raymond Sovey as her designer. Both Miss Latham and Professor Milton Smith continued to use the theatre-in-the-round technique for several years.

Another pioneer in this field was T. Earl Pardoe, who employed arena staging in 1922 at Brigham Young University in Utah. The technique achieved more renown when Gilmor Brown started directing plays in Pasadena, in 1924, in the center of a large room with a minimum of equipment. Five years later Mr. Brown built the Playbox, which is an intimate theatre, but is not solely devoted to theatre-in-the-round, for its three alcove stages and its staircase make it a rather flexible playhouse.

Theatre-in-the-round proper as an intimate theatre medium was instituted by Glenn Hughes in 1932, when he produced Ibsen's *Ghosts* in the center of the floor in a hotel penthouse in Seattle, Washington. The purpose of Hughes's theatre was to give his students an outlet for continuous performances and to provide more entertainment for Seattle's theatregoers. The venture was enormously successful, and in 1940, a new structure—the only one of its type in the world—was built on the campus of the University of Washington. It is known, in honor of its first home, as the Penthouse Theatre.

In the years to follow many college and community theatres found that theatre-in-the-round was a practical and interesting solution for their building problems. (Charles H. Gray, of the University of Houston, has prepared a graph, which appears in this book, showing the growth of the medium since 1914). The technique was also utilized in a summer theatre venture in the New York area by Jacob Weiser in the late thirties.

The first professional theatre-in-the-round in America was Theatre '50, which opened in Dallas, Texas, in the summer of 1947. Several other professional theatres of this type have been organized since then, and many more are rapidly springing up. There can be one in every city in the United States.

CHAPTER TWO

The Story of Theatre '50

My interest in the theatre started very early, although I was not quite aware of the fact that it was theatre. My father is a lawyer in Livingston, Texas, and until I was eleven years old I too wanted to be a lawyer. I used to sit in the courtroom and watch my father make speeches. I was in the presence of drama, but it took me some time to realize that. Then one day it occurred to me that the reason I enjoyed the courtroom sessions was that they were so much like plays. I must have been stage-struck even earlier, for my mother's scrapbook is full of pictures of me dressed up as something or other. But at eleven I knew what I wanted to do—to put on plays—and up went a sheet in the barn where my sister and my brothers joined me in my first producing-directing venture. I was lucky to know so early what I wanted to do. It gave me a valuable head start.

Until I was fourteen I did not have a chance to see a professional production of a play. New vistas opened to me when I watched Walter Hampden as Cyrano in Fort Worth, Texas. There are children all over our country who are as interested in the theatre as I was and who do not have the opportunity to see good theatre—another reason why I am adamant about the establishment of resident professional theatres.

I went to a girls' college (Texas State College for Women in Denton), where the drama courses were crowded with aspiring actresses, and I was the only student interested in directing. This was fortunate because I had a chance to direct much more than the average directing student in a drama department.

The college was close enough to Dallas so that I could see plays there very often. A great number of road companies hit Dallas in those years, and the old Dallas Little Theatre, one of the outstanding of its kind, was at its peak under the direction of Oliver Hinsdell. I saw many fine productions there.

I did a certain amount of acting in college plays, but always with the clear understanding that I was doing it to acquaint myself with the actor's viewpoint and problems, never with any ambition to become an actress myself. I did learn what it means not to get a part you are hoping for and how disappointing it is to get a walk-on when you expect the lead.

My desire to read plays was stimulated by one of my instructors, and I started to read a minimum of a play every day, a practice I have continued through the years, except that now I read mostly new scripts. But I remember lighting into the Greeks, Shakespeare, Ibsen, Chekhov, O'Neill as though they were my own personal discoveries and reading all their works.

Since no master's degree was offered in drama at my college at that time, I took it in psychology, but I managed to combine my interests by doing my thesis on "The Abnormal Ways Out of Emotional Conflict as Reflected in the Dramas of Henrik Ibsen," which consisted of case studies of Hedda Gabler (suicide), Ellida in *The Lady from the Sea* (hysteria), and Irene in *When We Dead Awaken* (insanity).

During one of the last seasons of my college life, I heard that a Texas drama critic was going to address a group of journalism majors. I did not belong to this group, but I knew he was going to speak about dramatic criticism, and I could not miss the lecture. An open forum followed his talk, and in the course of a discussion, the speaker asked me what I was interested in. I explained that I should not even be there, but I added, "I'm going to be a director." He said he would send me a little pamphlet on directing. He did, and the pamphlet, which I have always cherished, turned out to be Bernard Shaw's advice to directors. I mention this incident because for me it was a contact with the outside world, and the encouragement I was given by this critic helped me tremendously at that moment of my life.

I received my M.A. degree at eleven in the morning,

and that afternoon I was in Dallas knocking at the door of the newly formed Southwestern School of the Theatre (headed by Louis Veda Quince). I was applying for a job, and I was asked only one question, "Can you type?" Fortunately I had spent a couple of summers typing abstracts in my father's law office, so I could answer "yes." Although I was little more than a glorified office girl, I had an opportunity to watch the director of the School at work, and this experience was a source of real inspiration.

After a year in Dallas, and with my academic degrees under my belt, I wanted to gain an understanding of theatre all over the world. I thought the Pasadena Playhouse would be a step in the right direction. I enrolled in the Pasadena Summer School of the Theatre and was fortunate to be a member of an unusually adult group of students and to direct plays under the supervision of men of taste and ability. It is hard to know, as you look back, what influences were most important in forming you, but I do know that I was highly stimulated that summer. I was given encouragement, and I cannot say enough times that I feel that is what young people need above all—to have someone they respect in their field of endeavor to show faith in them.

The Pasadena summer course completed, I got my first directing job with the Ojai Community Players. Ojai, California, is a beautiful little valley, in which years later the Chekhov Players conducted their work. The theatre at

Ojai was already in existence when I was engaged, and while I cannot claim that I contributed to its development, I did direct *Hedda Gabler* that year. I have done this play twice since then, and I have discovered that it is possible for a director to find new values and a richer texture in a script every time it is approached anew.

Soon after my year at Ojai, I had an opportunity to take a trip around the world. It was a most valuable and fascinating experience. I went to the theatre every evening I was on shore—in Japan, China, India, England, France. I visited practically every large city in the world before I ever laid eyes on New York (my trip had originated on the West Coast). I arrived in New York the night Joe Louis knocked out Max Baer, and the Group Theatre was doing *Waiting for Lefty* as a curtain raiser for *Awake and Sing*. It was the fall of 1935. New York made me feel that I had to go to work for the present and plan the future. The theatrical air was exhilarating, and it filled my lungs.

While I was abroad, Federal Theatre had been started. When I heard about it on the boat coming back, it seemed logical to me to go to my home territory and participate in the enormous program Federal Theatre had mapped out.

I became assistant director of the Houston Federal Theatre, which was co-sponsored by the Houston Recreation Department, but it only lasted a few months. Hallie Flanagan, national director of Federal Theatre, wrote in her book *Arena,* "Texas was a hard nut to crack, and we failed to crack it." But while the program failed in Houston, there was much to learn about human reactions, about the plight of unemployed entertainers, about the activities of the Recreation Department in Houston.

Following the collapse of the Federal Theatre Project in Houston I went abroad again, this time to see the Moscow Art Theatre Festival, which I covered in a series of articles for *The Houston Chronicle.* On this trip I also saw Berlin and Warsaw and revisited London and Paris.

Upon my return the Houston Recreation Department offered me a job teaching playground directors to put on plays with children in the various parks of the city. I took the job because I had a feeling it would lead to something else. I knew I wanted to have a theatre of my own, and I saw no reason why I couldn't have it in Houston. I believed then what I believe now about the theatre and what it should be. Being an idealist, I thought my place was in the little-theatre movement which sought exciting experimentation. The broad flexibility of this term attracted me tremendously.

The Recreation Department had a small building with a stage which was being utilized for square dances on Wednesdays and Saturdays. I asked if I could have this house free of charge to produce plays provided I would do it without giving up my other duties. The moment I obtained permission to use the theatre, I announced in the papers that the Houston Community Players had been formed and that *The Importance of Being Earnest* was to be the first production. Nine people showed up for tryouts, and they filled the nine parts of the play. Six of them contributed one dollar apiece to finance the project, and we opened in December of 1936, charging twenty-five cents for admission. We ran two nights, but managed to get some attention and even one review in the press. I found out that when you have no money to do a show (although it is wonderful to be able to finance a production properly), you are *forced* to be ingenious; as a result, you can sometimes even be creative.

Our second production was Elmer Rice's *Judgment Day*. Since our theatre was being used for another purpose at the time, and I was determined not to postpone the second play, we performed *Judgment Day* in a courtroom, an ideal setting since the script dramatized the trial of the Reichstag Fire.

Getting *Judgment Day*—and later *Merrily We Roll Along*—on the stage cured me of ever again being frightened of large casts or numerous sets. Then we did *Hedda Gabler* and definitely attracted the attention of the Houston drama critics. We ended the first season with a highly stylized production of *Squaring the Circle*, which employed ladders, ropes, sawhorses and barrels, all painted a violent red and skeletonized against a black backdrop.

That summer I decided I had sufficient proof that we had an audience eager to see good plays. I offered to run the Community Players and make enough money to pay my own salary and production expenses. Six plays were planned for the second season, and we sold subscription tickets for two dollars each. The following season the Recreation Deapartment, pleased with the success of our theatre, put me on the city pay roll, which helped our financial setup because all we took in at the box office could be spent on the plays themselves.

I felt about my job in this community theatre in Houston as strongly as I did later when I directed plays on Broadway or when I established Theatre '50 in Dallas. It was just as important to me then as it is now to try to do fine plays in as exciting and excellent a way as I possibly could. I didn't do it with the thought that it would be valuable experience for my work ten years later, but in the belief that I had a job which had to be done well. My ambition was to make the Houston Community Players the most exciting theatre in America.

While our repertoire did include a number of plays which had been previously produced, I was becoming interested in the new script. The first original I did was *Special Edition* by Harold Young, a Houston city editor. I followed this with two original musicals, written by Cy Howard and Richard Shannon. We also did several one-act plays by Houston writers in laboratory productions. And we were especially proud to present the world premiere of Edwin Justus Mayer's play, *Sunrise in My Pocket.* I had first heard about this play and read it while visiting in Los Angeles, and I phoned Brooks Atkinson in New York asking him to introduce me to the author. Mr. Atkinson complied by telegraph, and I obtained the rights to the play. The experience of presenting this play was exhilarating, and it gave me new courage and incentive to go after new manuscripts.

The Houston Community Players also presented classics like *Macbeth, The Learned Ladies, The Master Builder, The Taming of the Shrew, Uncle Vanya, The Comedy of Errors and As You Like It.* Norris Houghton, who visited us in 1940 while gathering material for his book, *Advance from Broadway,* found that " . . . one of Margo's most provocative statements was: 'My most successful box-office productions have been the classics. I always have to sell standing room for Shakespeare, Ibsen or Chekhov.' " In comparing this statement to that of other community-theatre directors who insisted on a permanent fare of modern light comedies, he made a pertinent analysis concluding with these words:

"Is it perhaps that those dramas a director cares for most, and in which he consequently outdoes himself, are those which the public most heartily enjoys? May it not be possible that the reason the classics are not supported in some places is because they are not well-enough done, because *Margin for Error* and *What a Life are* given better productions than *Macbeth* or *The Master Builder?*"

It was during my association with the Houston Community Players that I was introduced to the theatre-in-the-round technique. In the spring of 1939, I went to Washington, D. C. for a theatre conference and saw a production by the Blue Room Players of Portland, Oregon, a group which had been formed by a disciple of Glenn Hughes. Their performance of a light comedy in a hotel ballroom impressed me so much that I felt I could do something similar in Houston. I remember that on the train on my way back to Houston I shocked the girl sitting next to me by springing up from my seat all of a sudden and exclaiming, "Why not?"

My theatre in Houston was too hot for summer productions and the cost of having it air-conditioned was prohibitive. Yet I wanted to be active the whole year round, and the answer seemed to be theatre-in-the-round. All I had to do was to persuade one of the hotels to give me an air-conditioned room on the mezzanine. I succeeded in this, and we produced six plays during the summer. This was my first direct experience with theatre-in-the-round.

In the meantime, the Houston Community Players had grown from nine actors in 1936 to some six hundred participants in the early 'forties. We had produced over sixty plays and had acquired fifteen thousand dollars' worth of equipment.

But in spite of this growth, during the last season I spent in Houston, I began to see the great necessity of rehearsing eight hours a day for at least a three-week period in order to be able to get a play on and feel thoroughly satisfied with the production. I also began to realize that if one wanted theatre at its best, it was essential to obtain the service of the most talented people available and to be in a position to dispense with their services if they were unable to do their jobs properly. Since in a community theatre it is only possible to work in the evenings, these requirements were an impossibility. I came to the conclusion that to satisfy the above-mentioned needs, the ideal working situation would have to be a permanent professional theatre.

The war had started. Life and time had become much more precious. Everybody realized the value of theatre as a source of both inspiration and relaxation, but more than ever the full time of theatre workers was required especially when many of our community theatre people started to leave for military duty. The war intensified in my mind the need for a professional theatre.

But wartime was not the logical moment for beginning action on such a theatre. While I went to direct a play at a summer theatre in East Hampton, I weighed the possibilities and decided that there was at least one type of theatre in which people were not leaving for war—or at least not all of them—the university theatre. My place at this time should be with the younger people who were being trained for the theatre of tomorrow. It so happened that there was a position available for me in the Drama Department of the University of Texas.

There I directed three new plays and worked on several theatre-in-the-round productions (including one of the new scripts). I also took a leave of absence from my academic duties to stage *You Touched Me*, a play by Tennessee Williams and Donald Windham, first at the Cleveland Playhouse (with Carl Benton Reid in the leading role) and then at Pasadena (with Onslow Stevens). When I went back to Pasadena in the summer of 1944, I directed Williams's *The Purification* and two other new scripts.

During my two years of university teaching and directing I started working very concretely towards a plan for a professional repertory theatre. I remember the date when the plan became very clear in my mind—December 7, 1943.

I had been coming to New York quite often and had been to California and had traveled all over the world. I had talked to writers, actors, directors, producers, critics—all the members of the wondrous fraternity of theatre people who meet and talk about their dreams and their ideals. And I had found out that everybody—including the wonderful people I met in the books theatre people had written—who had ideals was discussing the same thing: a way to have theatre, to establish the fine companies which could produce the kind of theatre we all dreamed of. I said to myself, "We dream beautifully, but what are we doing about it? Why do we keep talking? Do we enjoy conversation more than action? I can't believe that!" It was then that I adopted as my motto a phrase which may seem a little crude, but not too much so if you apply it only to yourself: "Put up or shut up."

And so, as 1943 was drawing to a close, I decided that my way in the theatre pointed to the formation of a permanent resident professional theatre with a repertory system, producing new plays and classics with an accent on the new script. How could it be done? I knew I had to find a place for it, and I knew it had to be a beautiful theatre which would give actors and other theatre people a place to work and audiences a place where they would be entertained and enlightened.

I wrote out a plan reasonably soon thereafter and started thinking in terms of a city where my theatre could be established. Somehow all the roads pointed to Dallas. It is practically in the middle of the country; it is in a new, fresh, rich, pioneering part of the nation; it is a city already rich in theatre tradition; it had always been a good road town; there were many sincere theatre lovers there who were anxious to help; I had gone to school near Dallas and had worked there; it was my home territory; Dallas at that moment was without a theatre of any kind and wanted one very badly. It was a logical choice for me.

I had spoken about my plan to John Rosenfield, drama editor and critic of the Dallas *Morning News,* and to a few other people in Dallas, and in one of our conversations Mr. Rosenfield said, "Why not here?" I was glad because I wanted it to be there. In the early spring of 1944, when the choice was made, Mr. Rosenfield was instrumental in having me meet people in Dallas who were interested in the project; from then on out the theatre was being planned for a specific city.

Now I needed time to look into the problems of finance and organization, availability of scripts and personnel and existing theatre buildings. With this in mind, I applied for a Rockefeller Foundation fellowship, outlining my program of travel and time to be spent in Dallas as follows:

"1. Getting as complete a picture as possible of the present American theatrical scene—from the point of view of the knowledge being of practical value in starting a professional theatre in Dallas. I should like to visit as many theatres as possible—professional and nonprofessional. I should like to talk to as many theatre people as possible. I should like to watch the best designers, lighting men, directors and all technicians at work. I should like at the end of the year to have at my finger tips as much new knowledge and inspiration as it is possible to get in a year.

"I would especially like to meet and talk to the young playwrights. I want to collect new scripts and read at least three plays a day during the year of work. I would like to be able to read all the books on the theatre that I have not yet had a chance to read. I want to talk to the authors of many theatre books I have read.

"I especially want to talk to some of the great and idealistic theatre people whose works have so long influenced me—Robert Edmond Jones, Eugene O'Neill and many others.

"2. I want to spend a long enough time in Dallas to begin to know the city. I want to know its people, its schools, libraries, museums, churches, clubs, etc. I want to use a definite number of months in Dallas to raise the funds. After this is done . . .

"3. I want to talk to all the young creative theatre people in the country I can meet and from them select a staff and company of twenty for the creation of a resident professional theatre in Dallas.

"4. I want at the end of the year to:

a. Have a theatre building ready to open.
b. Have a staff of twenty workers ready to go to work.
c. Have funds enough to provide these workers with security for the next ten years. (I can dream, can't I?)
d. Have new scripts, new ideas and new dreams enough to keep us all busy for one hundred years.

e. Have all the knowledge and wisdom I can possibly acquire in the year's time that will enable me to put this plan over in the way that it deserves."

Needless to say, I was expecting to accomplish too much within a year, but with slight variations, I did work towards the goals I had set for myself. The plan itself consisted of five points: finance and organization, personnel, plays and playwrights, theatre plant and the philosophy of such a theatre. These points will be discussed in detail in Chapter Three, but the preface to the plan can be quoted here:

"This is a plan for the creation of a permanent, professional, repertory, native theatre in Dallas, Texas: a permanent repertory theatre with a permanent staff of the best young artists in America; a theatre that will be a true playwright's theatre; a theatre that will give the young playwrights of America (or any country, for that matter) a chance to be seen; a theatre that will provide the classics and the best new scripts with a chance for good production; a theatre that will enable Dallasites to say twenty years from now, 'My children have lived in a town where they could see the best plays of the world presented in a beautiful and fine way'; where they can say, 'We have had a part in creating theatre and working in it; a theatre to go beyond the dreams of the past—and they have been wonderful; a theatre to mean even more to America than the Moscow Art meant to Russia, the Abbey to Ireland, or the Old Vic to England; a theatre that will carry on, but adapt to our country and time, the ideals of the Stanislavskys, the Copeaus, the Craigs; a theatre of our time."

Looking back on these words, I am certain that what I had in mind included the creation of similar theatres throughout the country, for I do not believe that in a country as large as ours one center could or should provide the whole nation with theatrical entertainment. It would be against the principle of decentralization, which holds true whether the center is located in New York or in Oregon.

The officers of the Rockefeller Foundation were very sympathetic towards my plan, and I obtained the fellowship in the summer of 1944. Since I had been directing at the summer session of the Pasadena Playhouse, I started my travels in the California area. Before I had a chance to cover much other territory, I was interrupted by a call from New York to co-direct Tennessee Williams's first Broadway production, *The Glass Menagerie.* It seemed to be the wisest procedure to discontinue the fellowship and go to New York, for it meant an opportunity to practice what I had been preaching—the gaining of experience in all fields of the theatre. And I realized that I needed the added training of the Broadway stage. Another strong consideration was the fact that I believed in Williams and loved the play. *The Glass Menagerie* opened in Chicago on December 26, 1944. The rest is history. It was wonderful and fortunate for me to have had my first Broadway experience with a great playwright and some of the finest theatre artists in America.

After *The Glass Menagerie* was launched, I returned to Dallas in order to start organizing the theatre. I was accompanied by Joanna Albus, who became my associate and worked indefatigably on the project, remaining with it through our first season.

Almost immediately after our arrival, Mr. and Mrs. Eugene McDermott gave the theatre the sum of ten thousand dollars as an organizational fund. A board of directors consisting of forty-eight citizens, with an executive committee of eleven, was formed at once; it was a good cross section of the city and large enough to be representative. The following day the theatre was incorporated under the laws of the State of Texas as a nonprofit professional repertory theatre, and an office was set up under the title of "Dallas Theatre, Incorporated."

A financial campaign was in order, but before raising money for a theatre, it is imperative to have a building. I canvassed the city and got well acquainted with the real estate situation. Our best chance seemed to be the Old Globe Theatre, which had been erected as a temporary building on the Fair Park grounds during the Texas Centennial for the use of Shakespearean players. Although the land of the Fair Park grounds is under the control of the city Park Department, the State Fair Association supervises all buildings and activities. We obtained permission from the Association with the approval of the Park Department to use the theatre, and proceeded to have it approved by the City Building Inspector and the Fire Department. The location was excellent, for the Fair Park grounds were quite a center of activity—symphony, light opera, football, aquarium and museum.

While the financial campaign to raise $75,000 for our theatre was officially starting, Jo Mielziner flew to Dallas to look over the Globe in order to plan the structural changes I needed to convert it into a flexible playhouse. Mr. Mielziner felt that it was unwise to put any money into such a temporary structure. He realized the circumstances, however, and took all the necessary measurements and blueprints and left for New York, but not before advising me to try once more to find a better building. I went back into the problem of the theatres we had investigated previously, but there were no possibilities outside of the Globe.

Soon after Mr. Mielziner's departure we received a letter from the Building Inspector listing a number of things that would have to be done to the building before it could be occupied. I sent a copy of these requirements to Mr. Mielziner, asking him if it would be possible to meet these conditions for a reasonable amount of money. He replied that it would be possible, but the cost would be considerably higher than we had originally estimated. Still, we had to have a playhouse, and we threw all our energies into the fund-raising activities.

And then, in the middle of this campaign, I was called into conference with the City Building Inspector and the Fire Department. The Globe building, I was informed, had been categorized as "No. 5 Type," which according to the law is out of question for a theatre building. This was a most discouraging piece of news because having our building condemned placed our whole financial campaign in a rather ridiculous light. But I had a comforting thought: the people on the board of directors and on the financial committee were behind me and continued to have faith in the project.

Our search for a theatre started again, although it seemed there was no place left to look. The war was drawing to a close, and the housing situation was terrible. To build a new theatre would have been inadvisable, even if we could have raised the money for it. But the project never stopped. The office kept on working.

I never left the project, but I did take two leaves of absence to come to New York to direct Maxine Wood's play, *On Whitman Avenue*, and later Maxwell Anderson's *Joan of Lorraine*. Then I returned to Dallas with the determination that the job had to be done and could not be delayed any longer.

"When there is no theatre available," I asked myself, "and yet you must start a theatre, what do you do?"

I had found the answer once before, when I wanted to produce plays in the summer in Houston. Why not the same answer now? It took a great deal of determination, for this was not the kind of theatre I had been talking about. But had I been talking about a building or about an idea? And couldn't the idea be applied just as well in theatre-in-the-round? It could. When one runs out of solutions, the unusual solution will save the day. The board of directors liked my suggestion, and we set out to look for a different type of building. The problem was easier, but not nearly as easy as it seems in retrospect.

We found a beautiful and charming building made of stucco and glass brick, a modern structure, air-conditioned, lovely to look at, well-equipped and adaptable to theatre-in-the-round. It was also located on the Fair Park grounds and had been leased by the Gulf Oil Corporation. We were allowed to occupy it free of any charge but the payment of utilities. After the Gulf Oil lease expired, we obtained it from the State Fair Association for a nominal fee. In the spring of 1947 all papers were signed with the approval of the State Fair Association and the City Park Department. Within twelve hours I flew to New York to get started. . . .

The building had to be put in shape, but plans had been made before we had the final approval, so we were ready to go to work on the building of platforms, installation of seats (which were loaned to us at first), carpeting and lighting equipment. We discovered that, to avoid impairing sightlines or comfort and to allow enough space for an adequate playing area, our maximum seating capacity had to be limited to 198. Our technical director, Joseph Londin (who had been engaged previously), had already conferred in New York with Jo Mielziner and with Edward Kook, of the Century Lighting Company; our setup had been blueprinted and was ready to be installed.

I planned a first season of ten weeks. I chose a short season because it seems extremely advisable to have before you start enough financing to insure the completion of a season.

During two years, my associates—Joanna Albus and June Moll—and I had been reading plays continuously. None of the other problems which confronted us ever stopped us from that one pleasurable duty. I knew what plays we wanted to do and proceeded to choose four new scripts and one classic for the first season. All I had to do in New York in this regard was to confer with agents and sign contracts.

But my first task in New York was to find a first-class business manager. I cannot overemphasize the importance of this job in a professional theatre setup. He must know the art and craft of managing a professional theatre; he must have experience, ability, a hard-boiled business sense. To have the respect of the town, the theatre must be run in as businesslike a fashion as a department store. I was very fortunate to find just the kind of person I was looking for in Manning Gurian.

I hired a company of eight actors, a number which at this time seemed more feasible than the twenty I had called for in my original plan. The business manager bought the actors their railroad tickets, and they arrived in Dallas three weeks prior to the opening.

In three weeks' time in New York I optioned four plays, hired a business manager and a company, while tickets and publicity and technical equipment were being prepared in Dallas. I would like to add that I could not have done this without the co-operation of unions, agents and other theatre people in New York; they can be wonderful friends when the occasion arises and make one proud and happy to be a part of the American theatre.

Theatre '47, as it was now called, opened on June 3, 1947, with William Inge's *Farther Off From Heaven.* With staggered rehearsals, we had three plays in preparation at the time we opened. Our repertory system, which has varied since then, meant that each of the five plays was repeated after a new opening, and the last two weeks of the season were devoted to a repertory festival. The purpose of the festival was to enable visitors from other cities and people in Dallas who had not seen some of the plays to view our work.

The season started slowly at first, but built continuously, catching momentum with the third production. As a whole, it was a fantastically successful first season. But the task is not accomplished once the theatre has opened. Productions have to be good; the standard has to be maintained and constantly raised. This means reading more plays, searching for good actors and technical improvements and working hard on public relations. It means that work is required morning, noon and night—and then some.

The name of our organization, suggested by a theatre in Prague, is changed every year on New Year's Eve in order to remain contemporary at all times. The audience that night is asked to attend the performance a little later than usual and to join the actors, after the play, in greeting the new year and the new name of the theatre.

Theatre '47 completed its season with enough funds to start Theatre '48 with a twenty-week plan. It was then that we decided we wanted three weeks of rehearsal for each play; Theatre '49, therefore, ran for thirty weeks, and Theatre '50 followed the same plan. As this book goes to press, Theatre '51 has hopes of presenting each play for a period of four weeks.

CHAPTER THREE

A Resident Professional Theatre: Where and How

The planning and organizing of a permanent resident professional theatre will vary according to the type of theatre building, but there is a basic procedure which I believe essential regardless of whether or not the structure is to include a proscenium arch and a stage. The purpose of this chapter is to outline this procedure, also pointing out some of the differences that would exist if theatre-in-the-round technique is to be used.

I have mentioned the plan which I submitted to the Rockefeller Foundation when I applied for a fellowship; although certain minor changes have occurred, I have never found it necessary to deviate from any of the basic principles of the original plan, and for this reason it still seems to be a good starting point. The plan was divided into five parts, as follows:

1. Organization and Finance
2. Personnel

3. Plays and Playwrights
4. Physical Plant
5. Philosophy

A discussion of each one of these topics will indicate how I believe a resident professional theatre can be started, but I would like to preface all the following remarks with one fundamental piece of advice to any theatre person who undertakes the establishment of such a theatre: the word *discouragement* must be eliminated from his vocabulary before he gets to work.

Organization and Finance

The first step is to draw up a plan, which will state what the ideals of the theatre are to be and how they can be carried out in practice. The aims and objectives of the theatre, its contribution to the American theatrical scene and to the community where it is to be located, the methods and techniques it will employ—all this must be included in the plan. It may be necessary to modify the plan after the theatre is started, but it is essential to have the basic ideas and ideals down on paper so that other people can become sufficiently interested in them to be of genuine assistance.

Deciding on a place is the next step. I believe that with willingness and determination and hard work a professional theatre can be opened in every town in the United

States. But it is undoubtedly true that, for the time being, it is simpler to do it in a large city, preferably with a population of one hundred thousand or more. Anyone who is going to attempt the organization of a theatre must know the city; if he does not, he should take the time to get thoroughly acquainted with it. It does not have to be your home town, but you must certainly have a general knowledge of the territory and a specific knowledge of the town. To a certain extent you will have to be guided by your inclinations. Any city is a good place to start a theatre; the only question is whether it is the best possible place for you. You must like the town, and the people in it must want you.

In every city there are people who are interested in a theatre project; if they do not find you, you must find them. Once you have established this relationship, the citizenry of the town will form a temporary organizational committee which will eventually expand into a board of directors. The board should be large enough to be representative of the city, but a small executive committee should also be maintained.

A decision has to be reached (unless this was already part of the plan) as to the method in which the theatre is to be financed. There are at least three possible ways:

1. The person who has drawn up the plan has the funds himself.

2. Capital is raised by selling shares as in any business.

3. Contributions are obtained for a nonprofit organization.

Naturally there are advantages and disadvantages in each one of these. Some theatre people cherish the dream of inheriting, earning or winning a large sum of money (say, for instance, $75,000) to open a theatre in the city of their choice. This would eliminate the fund-raising campaign, and the theatre could open more rapidly; on the other hand, it would be less of a civic venture, and the town, not having participated in the financing of the theatre, might not feel as much a part of it. Still, I believe that if someone has the money and has the right ideals, he should get started without delay.

A resident professional theatre could also be financed along the same lines as a production in the commercial theatre; that is, a number of people invest a determined sum with the hope of making a profit. This method makes continuity very problematic in the theatre, unless the first production is successful at the box office. We know that on the Broadway scene it is considerably easier for a producer to raise money if his last few shows have been hits than if he has had even one or two failures in recent seasons. If the investment method is to be used, the backers must understand from the beginning that a resident theatre is a long-term project and that all profits cannot be taken out of the organization lest it be hard to continue and impossible to improve. However, as long as there is a thorough awareness on the part of the management and the investors that the standards cannot be lowered in order to make more money, there is nothing wrong with this method.

Theatre '50, as I have already stated, is a nonprofit corporation which we have found to be both sound and workable. Unlike many nonprofit organizations, a theatre should and can make enough money to pay for itself, provided an initial sum is raised to start it.

The most obvious advantages of the nonprofit system are: there is no temptation on the part of the management to reduce the standards in order to earn larger profits; the staff and company have security and permanence; donations are deductible from income tax, and there are certain other small tax leniencies.

In order to be incorporated as a nonprofit organization and obtain a state charter, it is necessary to show high ideals and objectives which will be of cultural and educational value.

A theatre building must be acquired before a detailed budget can be outlined. It is imperative to know what type of building is available, its seating capacity, whether it will require remodeling, what kind of lighting equipment it will need, its rental and operation costs. Since finding a building can become one of the major problems in organizing a theatre, one solution is to decide on theatre-in-the-round technique. It will still be necessary to find a place, but the problems are greatly simplified.

The budget should be prepared by a first-class business manager in consultation with the managing director. It should cover all expenses necessary to open the theatre and to operate it for a first season. When the budget is ready, you know how much money has to be raised. Theatre '50 found a $40,000 fund satisfactory, but perhaps, if the management knows from the start that it will operate a theatre-in-the-round, certain unnecessary preliminary expenses can be avoided, and the theatre can open after raising a fund of $25,000. My estimate is that an excellent theatre-in-the-round can be started in any city in the United States with a sum between $25,000 and $40,000. A theatre can be opened on much less, but not if it is to have high standards.

To obtain the money, a professional fund-raising campaign must be set up. Just as a director would not allow a financier to stage his plays, he should not assume that he can do the financier's job. A financial committee of outstanding citizens is appointed by the board of directors (in our case we had a committee of six), and the chairman should be someone who is thoroughly familiar with this type of work (our chairman was Mr. DeWitt Ray, president of the National City Bank of Dallas). The fund-raising campaign must be professionally conducted by a paid staff; it has to be as sound, businesslike and civic as the Community Chest or symphony orchestra fund-raising programs.

After the money is raised, the management can proceed to sell subscriptions for the first season. Subscribers in our theatre pay the same price as individual ticket holders ($2.50 for evening performances and $1.80 for matinees). They have the first choice of seats and, by purchasing season tickets, enable us to plan a better program. A small list of subscribers for the initial season should not be a disappointment to the management; it is only reasonable to expect the list to grow as the theatre begins to prove itself through actual performances. In the last two seasons we have found a practical device to obtain subscriptions. In spite of the fact that I do not believe speeches should be made in the theatre, I make this one exception because it saves time and trouble for both theatregoer and management. During the showings of the last production in the spring, the managing director asks the audience to turn their programs to an order blank for next season's subscription and suggests that they fill it out at once if they are interested (a pencil has been placed under the arm of each seat). Subscribers are not billed until fall, and they have the privilege of changing the day of the week on which they want to attend.

While subscriptions are being obtained for the first season, a publicity campaign is organized, tickets are printed, and, most important of all, a staff and an acting company are selected and engaged. But before turning to this matter, I want to discuss the costs of operating a resident professional theatre.

The Budget

Opening the theatre for the first time involves certain costs which will not occur again. Like all other items, the expenditures at this time will vary; what is most important to remember is that the initial amount raised must include the costs of opening the theatre and of operating it for one season, preferably a short one.

Every effort must be made to acquire or rent a building for as low a rate as possible, because this item can wreck the entire budget. In the case of Theatre '50, for the first three seasons the Gulf Oil Company gave us our building free of rent (we paid maintenance only). After the Gulf Oil Company gave up its lease, the building reverted to the State Fair Association which allowed us to use it for a low nominal fee.

The largest expenses to equip the building as a theatre (since I am using Theatre '50 as an example, this applies primarily to a theatre-in-the-round) are the platforms, the seats and the installation of the lighting equipment.

The building of our platforms cost approximately

$3,000, and they were made and installed so as to make the room look as if it had been built to be a theatre. Less permanent platforms may be used, but they tend to give a makeshift appearance to the whole playhouse.

It is highly advisable to use regular theatre seats; they are expensive but they are worth it. New ones cost between $15 and $20 apiece, but secondhand seats in good condition can be purchased for as little as $7 per seat. Theatre '50 was fortunate to obtain its theatre seats as a gift.

The lighting and sound equipment, including the construction of the canopies, cables, switchboard, turntables, amplifiers, lights and installation, will cost a theatre-in-the-round setup between $3,000 and $5,000.

Carpeting has to be provided for the entire playing area as well as for the aisleways up to the entrances; we used inexpensive carpeting and limited the cost to $500.

Dressing rooms must be equipped with lavatories, lights and mirrors. If the building does not have a box office, arrangements must be made for one; the same applies to rest rooms and a cloakroom.

In addition to these expenses, an organizational fund is necessary to pay the salaries of a small staff (we had two people working all the time prior to the opening of the theatre, and at times three), preliminary expenses for stationery, mailing of manuscripts, publicity and promotion for the financing campaign. The amount required for an organizational fund will vary with the time needed before the theatre can start operating, and the person undertaking the establishment of a theatre must either have or promote this amount.

There are also certain expenses made every year prior to the opening of the season. These include:

1. Option money for plays; this is an advance against the author's royalties. Since we usually option five new plays for a season, the amount is $750.

2. Transportation of actors and production staff from wherever they are (usually New York) to wherever the theatre is located. The amount will vary with the distance; we spend between $1200 and $1500 on this item. The return trip is prorated in the weekly operating costs.

3. The treasurer's salary during the months the theatre is closed between seasons; the treasurer is the one person who stays on the job the year round in order to keep the business office running at all times.

4. Publicity and promotion, including the printing of folders announcing the season as well as tickets and envelopes.

Between $10,000 and $15,000 have to be spent every year before opening the season, and this amount must, of course, come from the receipts of the previous season. Undoubtedly a season could be started on less money, but not as well as it should be.

Once the season has started, there should be a weekly budget, as follows (this is an example of our tentative weekly budget):

Actors' Salaries	$ 600.00
Staff Salaries (including director, assistant director, business manager, technical and costume directors, treasurer, production assistants, porter and maid)	710.00
Unemployment Tax	40.00
Production Expenses	250.00
(If a play runs for three weeks, it means we have a budget of $750 for its production; since, however, most plays are done in repertory, the production budget can be as high as $1250. The cost per play varies, but we maintain the weekly average.)	
Royalty (when doing new plays, and estimated at capacity)	150.00
Newspaper and other advertising	140.00
Public Relations (Salary of publicity director plus expenses)	125.00
Rentals (theatre and office)	51.25
Utilities (phone, lights, gas, fuel oil)	32.50
Miscellaneous	
Bookkeeper	12.50
Secretarial work	30.00
Insurance	25.00
Return railroading prorated	40.00
General	18.75
TOTAL	$2,225.00

This weekly amount fluctuates, but it is a fair tentative figure for a theatre with about two hundred seats. For a first season, however, I would consider this budget much too high and would limit it to a maximum of 60% of capacity business (in our case, about $1800).

A theatrical organization must keep three different accounts: (1) the master account; that is, funds left over from the preceding season, (2) the operating account: funds from sales of season tickets and individual tickets sold in advance, and (3) the tax account.

The moneys in the second account are not used until the customer has used his ticket; that means that this fund is never touched for operating expenses. The season is started with the funds available in the master account. At the end of each week, the amount of money represented by the number of season tickets used and individual tickets purchased is transferred into the master account and becomes available for operating expenses, after deducting the sum required for taxes which is deposited in the tax account. It is important to remember that although the theatre controls the funds once a season ticket is sold, it cannot really consider this money its own until the theatregoer has seen the play; this process is as automatic as breathing if a theatre has sound business management.

The following list of our operating disbursements for the 1948-49 season gives a summarized view of the total yearly expenditures:

Salaries (Direction, Management and Production)	$26,201.00
Salaries—Actors	21,075.00
Transportation of Company	2,664.23
Taxes—Employees' Unemployment Compensation	884.12
Costumes—Materials and Labor	7,700.11
Props, Scenery and Sundry Production Expenses	1,317.07
Royalties	1,663.22
Advertising and Promotion	8,547.36
Office Supplies and Secretarial Service	1,936.79
Office Rent	1,875.00
Program Printing and Commissions	3,735.24
Ticket Printing	592.82
Insurance—Property and Employees' Compensation	1,483.90
Building Repairs and Maintenance	932.01
Heat, Light and Water	700.38
Storage and Drayage	556.74
Telephone and Telegraph	696.32
Audit	400.00
Dues and Subscriptions	25.00
TOTAL OPERATING DISBURSEMENTS	$82,986.31

Personnel

Once the theatre is in operation, the board of directors should not be burdened with the everyday problems of the organization. The board represents the confidence of the citizenry of the town. The board hires the managing director and leaves policy making and the operation of the theatre in his hands.

The board meets twice a year. At the beginning of each season a financial and artistic report is submitted by the management along with plans for the ensuing season. The other meeting is held after the season is over, at which time the managing director and the business manager report on the year's accomplishments.

In the case of Theatre '50, the board of directors did not happen to hire the managing director because I had come to them with the plan, but it is in a position to discharge the managing director at any time when the board feels that he is not fulfilling his responsibilities.

Members of the board can be consulted when special problems arise, but it is advisable for the management to keep in mind that the people on the board are busy men and women who have professions and businesses of their own and they will be most helpful if they are called upon only when genuinely needed.

The managing director and the theatre director can be—and in the case of Theatre '50 are—one and the same person. This, however, is not essential. Eventual division of directorial duties will become necessary, and I believe that a variety of directorial approaches is healthy for a theatre. In planning for the future, it is advisable to think in terms of adding other directors to the staff and training them within the group itself.

The managing director is the over-all policy maker and planner. He reports to the board of directors twice a year, selects the plays as well as the rest of the staff and the acting company, and, with the co-operation of the staff, solves all problems confronting the organization. He must be able to delegate authority in order to keep the theatre moving at all times. Good leadership depends largely on finding the right people to work with.

The business manager together with the managing director prepares the budget and handles all moneys coming in or going out (bills, taxes, tickets, etcetera). It is the responsibility of the business manager to see that the management stays within the budget, at all times keeping the standards as high as possible. An efficient and professionally experienced person is necessary to fill this position; he must know the theatre thoroughly and understand its artistic aims; it is helpful if he is familiar with banking and law.

The publicity director is in charge of all public relations, including all forms of advertising and publicity. It is essential that the publicity director have a complete understanding and knowledge of the city and its activities.

The treasurer handles the box office and all matters pertaining to ticket sales. Tact and graciousness are as important as the more technical qualifications for this job. A patron has to be treated just as graciously when he is told that the house is sold out as when his order is accepted for available seats.

The assistant director and production manager (two jobs which we have combined) acts in the capacity of assistant to the director and for him when the director is absent; he is also the over-all co-ordinator of all productions.

The technical director of our theatre is the lighting designer and works with the director and costume director on the over-all visual production, which includes obtaining furniture and building or supervising the building of anything needed in the way of scenery. Since our theatre has a small staff, the technical director also executes the lighting and operates the switchboard, at times with the help of a production assistant.

The costume director designs the costumes, buys materials, sews or supervises the sewing of all costumes, always working very closely with the director and technical director. In our theatre all costumes are made on the premises, and I recommend this policy because it saves an enormous amount of time for the actors to have fittings in the same building where they rehearse.

Theatre '50 employs three of four production assistants who work with the heads of the different departments and help with lights, furniture and props. They are all members of Equity and, whenever necessary and possible, they are given parts in a play.

Our acting company consists of eight or nine; it is a small company because our operating cost is low. Obviously a playhouse with a larger seating capacity would allow for an increased budget and, therefore, a larger company. A group of sixteen actors would be ideal, for then almost any play could be cast within the company.

In order to present first-class professional theatre, it is very important to find actors with the right qualities. They must have talent, of course, but their talent must be matched by character. An extremely gifted actor whose temperament will cause continual friction in a company can ruin a whole season and harm the theatre more than any of his brilliant performances can contribute to the elevation of artistic standards. The ideal is to have extraordinarily talented people of fine character.

When you search for a company, you have to look for a perfect chemical combination: people who will work together, all of them feeling that they can express themselves well in this theatre and having mutual respect for each other. Although I feel that the primary consideration of all is what the spectator sees and hears when the lights go up, I do not believe you can give your audience exciting productions unless everybody in the cast and those backstage are happy working together.

In addition to talent and character, in a repertory

theatre flexibility is also essential. For this reason it is advisable to select actors with experience, yet not forgetting that there is new talent continuously arriving on the theatrical scene. You must believe enough in new talent to give it a chance; for, if every theatre would take only experienced actors, where would the experienced actors of tomorrow come from?

Since most of our experienced actors are on or around Broadway, and most of our younger talent is attracted towards the same center because it is the only place which has consistently provided the possibility of jobs in the theatre, at the present time almost all casting is done in New York. The director, however, should try to see as many plays as possible all over the country and continually find new sources of talent. We must remember that if we are to have great actors, we will have to create some of them, and I know of no better way than to give them an opportunity to play eight different roles during one season.

By what method is the director going to select the company? This is no simple matter. The first time I cast a play in New York, I was determined to see absolutely every actor who wanted an interview. But I discovered, much to my regret, that this was a physical impossibility; if I saw everybody, I would never get my own job done. I know that it seems paradoxical to young actors that, although producers are constantly screaming for new talent, it is difficult to see these people when they are actually casting a play. If the young actor will stop and analyze the situation, he will realize that the producer *does* see actors, but he sees only those whose work he knows or who have been highly recommended to him. It is, therefore, essential for the young actor to find a place for himself. If he would become part of a group or help to organize a producing unit, he would be investing his time and his energy much more profitably than walking the streets in the Broadway vicinity hoping for something next to a miracle. There is no denying that occasionally an actor gets a part simply by walking into an office at the right moment, but these instances are the exceptions. I say these things because I know how hard it is for the actor as well as I know what problems the director faces when he has to find the right people quickly.

If it is virtually impossible to see every actor, how, then, will the director find the best people for his theatre? I know of four possible ways:

1) You really know an actor's potential only if you have worked with him previously; you know his character and his ability. But this method would obviously limit your choice.

2) If you have seen an actor in a number of plays, preferably in a variety of roles, you will have an index to his talent. You will have to depend on an interview for your knowledge of his character, and I might add that a director should learn to be a good judge of character. Should it not be possible to see the actor in more than one

part, this is better than nothing, but it is not an absolute indication of his ability.

3) The actor is recommended to you by someone he has worked under and whose judgment you respect.

4) For people who do not fit into the above categories, it will be necessary to hold auditions. This group will include actors sent to you by reliable agents, actors who write to you directly and whose qualifications arouse your interest and a few inexperienced people whom you can only judge in this manner.

I have used all four methods to find the actors I wanted, but I believe that there is no real substitute for the first two: knowing the actor's work personally or having seen him on the stage.

Another consideration a director has to keep in mind when casting for a whole season is the relation of the actor to each one of the plays selected. It follows that actors in a resident repertory theatre must have a wide age range. Although my casting plans vary somewhat every season according to the plays to be done, the following distribution of actors is what I generally try to find:

A) Three women
   1. One who can play from the ages of 16 to 28 (usually the actress is in her early twenties).
   2. One who can play from 23 to 38 (the actress being around 30).

3. One with the widest range of 38 to 80.

B) Five men

1. One young leading man who can play from 24 to 35. If he can play a juvenile too, it is an added advantage; however, I have found that a juvenile is not essential as a permanent member of such a small company; if one is needed for a play and the young leading man cannot play him, he can be found outside the company.
2. A leading man whose age range is between 30 and 40 to play romantic leads as well as older parts. (Plays often call for two leading men.)

3 and 4. Two fairly young character men who can be extremely flexible and can play at least between 30 and 45, but preferably have an even wider range. (Frequently they will play such key roles as Malvolio and Sir Toby Belch.)

5. A character man who can play from 40 to 80.

In plays with larger casts we call on our production assistants to fill certain roles. If still more people are needed, we use students from near-by colleges; most students of acting are more than eager to gain this professional experience, and sometimes they may eventually become regular members of the company. We always maintain the required proportion of Equity members, however, and abide by all Equity rules.

There should be a way in which a resident professional theatre could channel inexperienced talent. Theatre '50 has no apprentices because we have not found a method altogether satisfactory for us. Having apprentices who pay in order to work in your theatre can become a form of exploitation on the part of the management; it is psychologically difficult for the apprentice and if he feels that he is being exploited, his spirits may be dampened by the experience.

In my original plan I included a school as part of the theatre, but I have found that conducting classes would be highly impractical for us. We are a one-hundred-percent production organization, and we have a small staff. A school would take the time and the energy of the staff away from the plays, and our primary aim is to give the city a fine theatre. In the plans we make for the future, however, we want to include the training of young actors.

The eight or nine actors in the company sign regular Equity contracts equivalent to those used for summer stock. They are paid $75.00 a week, including the initial rehearsal weeks, plus their transportation to Dallas and back. The production assistants receive $50.00 per week.

Since the director will strive for ensemble acting in a resident theatre, it is a good policy to retain certain actors for a number of seasons. On the other hand, there is virtue in new faces and new talents, too. We have found that a nice balance is brought about automatically, some actors remaining for several seasons and others for only one.

Plays and Playwrights

When I was a student at the Pasadena Playhouse, I remember going to a class of Gilmor Brown's in which he gave us a list of plays (which I considered very obscure at the time because I did not know them) and asked if any of us had read them. No one had. Mr. Brown made no further comment about this matter, but he succeeded in arousing my curiosity enough to go to the library and start searching for the plays. Months later I had an occasion to ask him for the reason behind his procedure, and he explained that there are many fine plays which have had successful long runs in the history of the theatre and have great literary and dramatic value, yet few of us know anything about them.

I tell this story because it is dangerous to become smug about the number of plays one has read. No one can cover all the fine plays of the past and the present in a lifetime of reading. And how can you know about a play unless you read it? How can you fall in love with it? Having read a play once is not enough either, if it is a matter of considering it for production. You have to read it again and again; and if you want to do classics, you should be in a constant process of reacquainting yourself with them. Only by doing this can you discover these plays anew and fall in love with them in relation to the moment and your theatre and your present company.

To have a great theatre we must have great plays, and to have them we must find them. We have the classics, of course, and these should be presented to the audience because they represent great creations of the past which are still great and exciting theatrical experiences today.

But, then, we must show them the plays of today. We must find these plays, and we must produce them. My policy at Theatre '50 is to do strictly new plays and classics, with emphasis on the new script, and I believe that this would be a wonderful policy for every theatre in the country.

My attitude towards the new script is one of wonderment. I always expect to find a great play when I open a manuscript. I have no sympathy with producers or directors who complain about the amount of reading they have to do. I do not care if I am deluged with plays; there are never enough to find among them the ones a director really wants to do. I think it is an obligation and a responsibility to read new plays and to read them with great care. The plays are there. It is up to us to discover them.

If even one moment in the play shows a spark of

talent, the author should be encouraged with at least a certain amount of praise in a letter from the director. You will get many plays which will seem bad to you, but not all of these will seem bad to everybody else. There is a tremendous difference of opinion because there is an inevitable subjective bias in evaluating a play, and a play you believe to be poor may be liked by another director or producer. But even if you are positive, beyond the shadow of a doubt, that you have read a terrible script, I believe a form letter of rejection is preferable to an analysis which will tell the playwright how hopeless his work is. You may not know the conditions under which he is writing, his age, his stage of development. It is not impossible that a man who submits a hopeless script today may turn out to be a fine playwright fifteen years from now. No one has the right to discourage a potential talent. A director has to remember that his own state of mind may affect his opinion of a play and sometimes it is advisable to re-read a script.

You must respect the playwright. He has worked hard to write his play, and when he sends it to you, he is waiting for an answer. Your responsibility to him (or to his agent or representative) in this respect has no connection whatsoever with the quality of his play. Common courtesy obliges you to have a system of handling manuscripts.

The actual procedure is to acknowledge receipt of the play on the day it arrives. If possible, the author should be given an estimate of how soon he can expect a reading. You will invariably get behind on your playreading, especially in the midst of a season, but it *is* possible to give the playwright an approximate date. Also, when the play arrives, a card is made out with the name of the script, the author, where it came from and the date of arrival.

After the script is read, a report is prepared, including the title, name af the author, agent if any, number of sets, size of the cast, a summary of the play and an appraising comment. All reports are filed in a loose-leaf book under the title of the play.

When the script is ready to be sent back to the author, a notation is made on the original card as to date when returned and the method (by hand, mail, express, etc.). You must not hang on to plays, for they are valuable to the playwright regardless of what you think of their quality; aside from the intrinsic values it may have for him, he has gone to the expense of having it typed and usually the number of copies in his possession is fairly small.

If you like the play but are not quite sure that you want to do it, you should write to the author and ask him if you may keep it for consideration, giving him some idea of how long you would like to hold on to it. It is better to make up your mind at once, but if you cannot, do not delay returning the manuscript without consulting the author first. And you must be very careful not to get his hope up unless you are fairly certain that you will decide to produce the play.

Once you have selected a play, there is no reason to postpone action. An option is taken, and we have found the Dramatists' Guild stock try-out contract the most advisable form to follow. The author is paid an advance of $150 against a royalty of 5% of the gross. This amount will enable the playwright to be present at the rehearsals and production of his play.

If the theatre can possibly afford to have a resident playwright on the staff, it is a highly desirable arrangement. In planning ahead for the expansion of the theatre, it seems imperative to me to include at least one resident playwright and, in time, more.

Physical Plant

While I believe that the idea must come before the building, we must not forget that the building and its facilities should match the conception of the theatre. It should be functional, comfortable and beautiful. It should be in harmony with the high ideals of your theatre and the fine quality of the productions. It is true that a great play can be enjoyed by an audience sitting on hard benches in a stuffy, hot room, but how much more they will appreciate it if they are comfortably seated in an air-conditioned theatre! New scientific discoveries and materials are being used in industry and in the home, but very few of them have reached the theatre. Developments in architecture, in lighting, in acoustics are as creative and important to the theatre as wonderful plays and fine performances.

When you do build a theatre, you should avail yourself of professional advice; no playhouse should be erected without the presence of a theatre consultant who has a knowledge of the new developments and ideas in theatre architecture. A fine theatre building does not have to be huge, nor does it have to be tremendously expensive, but it should have an exciting conception. Some of our finest theatre artists—among them Norman Bel Geddes, Robert Edmond Jones, Kenneth MacGowan, Lee Simonson, Jo Mielziner, Mordecai Gorelik—have been working in this direction. Their ideas and plans should be carefully studied before any building is undertaken.

The location of the theatre building has to be considered, too. There must be enough parking space in the vicinity, and it must be as accessible as possible. The exterior should match the beauty and comfort of the interior and its productions.

A repertory theatre is in constant use; for this reason, I do not think it should share its building with other organizations and activities such as visiting road companies or symphony orchestras. A permanent repertory theatre is continuously occupied by the company, either in performance or in rehearsal.

Because of the present economic situation, seemingly the most practical type of theatre to use is theatre-in-the-round, and in the following chapter its requirements will be outlined in detail.

Philosophy

Neither the building, nor the organization, nor the finest plays and actors in the whole world will help you create a fine theatre if you have no consistent approach of your own, a true philosophy of the theatre.

Why decentralization? Why a resident professional company? Why permanent? Why only new plays and classics? An explanation of all the answers is not sufficient; you must believe in them and believe in them passionately.

I believe that, as a result of theatre, life can be better. A doctor is good in proportion to how well he can help his patients to recover their health. A theatre person is good in proportion to the inspiration, amusement, beauty and education he can give to others. I want for other people what I want for myself: to live life to its fullest, to see good plays, to read great books, to see great paintings, to hear fine music, and so on with all the fine experiences the world offers. I believe that children in every community should grow up with the opportunity to see the great plays of the past and the present because it will make life more exciting for them. Both the people in the theatre and their audiences can live more lives through the theatre; their experience can be fuller and their understanding, too. This leads to greater progress.

I do not believe anyone should be satisfied with the second best. And we in the theatre must help to make it great by realizing all the potentialities of the playwright, the architect, the actor, the technician. With more great theatre, great art, great music throughout the world, life is bound to be better.

CHAPTER FOUR

Techniques of Theatre-in-the-Round

The Theatre Plant

A theatre-in-the-round can be started, generally speaking, in any room or tent or place large enough to seat an audience and leave enough space for a playing area. There are considerable differences of opinion as to the ideal shape, size, playing-area dimensions, seating arrangement and equipment for such a theatre; many workable setups, however, have been established, and since they are possible models for other theatres-in-the-round or at least springboards for new ideas, I will describe some of them.

Everything that has been said about the qualifications of any theatre applies to theatre-in-the-round as well; it must look and feel like a theatre, both inside and outside. If it is located within another building, every effort should be made to provide it with a separate entrance or with a marquee of its own.

There is only one building in America which has been erected expressly for the purpose of housing a theatre-in-the-round (but as this book goes to press, another is being completed in Houston, Texas). This is the Penthouse Theatre at the University of Washington in Seattle, founded and directed by Glenn Hughes. In his book, *The Penthouse Theatre,* Mr. Hughes describes it as: ". . . situated on an elevation overlooking Lake Union, surrounded by beautiful landscaping . . . a white, one-story building with an elliptical, dome-roofed central unit, and with rectangular wings. Its dimensions are 112 by 84 feet. It is of frame construction, and the exterior is weatherproof plywood. The interior is plastered throughout. Its design, which might well be termed modern classic, is purely functional." The size of the playing area, 12 by 18 feet, was arrived at by searching for the ideal dimensions of a drawing-room rug; the shape was determined because Mr. Hughes wanted to swing the audience around the stage and yet felt that a perfect circle would be "uninteresting and ill-adapted to the representation of a drawing-room."

The Penthouse Theatre seats 172 spectators and has three rows of seats, each raised six inches, the playing area being eighteen inches below the level of the foyer.

The nine-foot-wide foyer surrounds the entire auditorium and is equipped with two crescent-shaped, enclosed rooms which are fitted to the curves of the auditorium walls and serve as waiting rooms for the actors.

The box office, check room and one rest room are set into the curved façade. One of the wings, with square corners and a separate outside entrance, holds the furniture and property rooms; the other one, two large dressing rooms. The kitchen and the second rest room are in the corners on either side at the back. The heating and ventilating equipment is located in a small basement under the furniture room.

The lighting equipment is placed between the ceiling and the outer roof. There are forty holes in the ceiling, each approximately four inches in diameter; thirty-two of them cover the playing area and eight the audience. Above each hole there is a spotlight with either a Fresnel lens or an ellipsoidal reflector, adjusted to achieve a focal joint at the ceiling hole. The spots, which have lamps averaging 400 watts, are hooked in circuits of four units each.

One of the most interesting projects for a theatre-in-the-round (although it has never been built) is Norman Bel Geddes's design known as Theatre Number 14, which is described in *Architecture for the New Theatre:* "The stage is designed on the same principle as a European circus or a boxing ring, is circular and in the center of the building. Separating the stage from the auditorium are steps which form an apron and an approach to the stage for actors." The dressing rooms are on the ground floor, under the auditorium, and "radiate from a passage around the stairs leading to the assembly room and the stage."

The auditorium, which surrounds the stage, seats eight hundred, has six rows and no balcony. "It is cut by eight transverse aisles, but each tier of seats becomes an aisle by reason of the wide interval—four and one-half feet—between one chair back and the next. By this arrangement each seat has plenty of leg room and also commands an excellent view of the entire stage.

"Surrounding the auditorium is a broad promenade with windows. Projecting from the promenade is an upstairs lounge, at either side of which are retiring rooms. An outdoor terrace is cantilevered above.

"The basement, where all scene changes are made, contains storage space for scenery and properties. The scenery is set on two movable stages which are raised and lowered by hydraulic power. In their elevated position at the auditorium level, they form the acting stage floor. One stage is being set while the other is being 'played'; the substitution, which takes a few seconds, is made behind a curtain of light or a moment's blackout. The stage, when lowered, descends, into a shallow pit which brings its floor level with the basement floor. This stage is then carried from its original position to one side, a distance equal to its diameter, on tracks. The second stage, already set for the next scene, is automatically rolled into position and raised to the auditorium level.

"Surrounding the dome that spans both stage and auditorium are two concentric light galleries with locations for lamps at many angles. All lamp positions are invisible to the audience as seated during the performance. Inside the railing in front of the first row of seats is a circular row of lamps for throwing light upward (as footlights do on a proscenium stage). All lights are controlled from a single switchboard. The over-all diameter of the auditorium, including the promenade, is 132 feet, and that of the circular stage 30 feet. The longitudinal axis of the theatre is 300 feet. From the stage floor to the peak of the dome above is 65 feet. The basement is 25 feet below the ground level.

"The administrative offices are on the ground floor and consist, at the front, of entrance foyer, box offices, manager's office, producer's offices. At the rear of the building are the green room, director's office, stage manager's office, stage-door entrance, a waiting room and the freight elevator entrance."

The Lambertville Music Circus, organized in 1949 by St. John Terrell, consists of a tent (130 feet by 96) which covers a circular bowl, dug expressly for this purpose. The height of the tent is approximately 45 feet from the center of the stage. The audience is seated around an elliptical raised platform (26 feet by 19) and the orchestra is in a pit at one side of the stage. The lights are fastened to the poles which hold the tent up. When it originally opened, the Music Circus had a seating capacity of one thousand, but since then it has been enlarged to thirteen hundred. Permanent seats cannot be installed in a tent, but the Music Circus uses very comfortable canvas chairs.

The Penthouse Theatre of Atlanta, Georgia, is located on the top floor of the Ansley Hotel in a room which was formerly a night club. It has an almost square stage, the dimensions being 25 feet by 22, and the seating capacity is 450. The founders of this theatre, Don Gibson and Elsbeth Hofmann, have also started a similar venture in Jacksonville, Florida.

Also located in a hotel, but on the ground floor, is the Arena Theatre in New York City, which opened in the summer of 1950 under the management of David Heilweil and Derrick Lynn-Thomas. Its auditorium is a former ballroom of the Hotel Edison, provided with a separate entrance and a marquee. The seating capacity is five hundred. The dimensions of the rectangular platform stage are 18 feet by 14, with four aisleways leading to it; the playing area is lit by forty 500-watt leico lights.

Theatre '50 has a seating capacity of 198, determined by the size of our building. There is no proof yet as to what the perfect size of a theatre-in-the-round should be, but we do know that one of the great virtues of this type of staging is its intimacy, and this quality must be maintained. I believe that the seating capacity can be easily increased to five or six hundred without impairing the intimacy of the playhouse. If the seating arrangement is very carefully planned, it seems, however, that it can be as large as eight hundred (as in Norman Bel Geddes's design) or thirteen hundred (as in the Lambertville Music Circus).

Theatre '50 has three rows of seats on two sides of

the house, and four and five, respectively, on the other two. Bel Geddes indicates six rows in his design, and it seems to me that this is the maximum number in a playhouse in which there is sufficient space between the playing area and the first row. Where the first row touches the playing area, it is possible to have seven or eight rows, but there will be a spill of light on a portion of the audience.

Also, in order to maintain the intimacy, I believe the first row of seats should be on the same level with the playing area. In some theatres either the first row or the stage has been placed on a platform; experiments have also been made to separate the actors from the audience with scrims or fences. But I have learned that the audience, when it comes into a theatre-in-the-round, finds the idea of being in the same room with the actors one of the chief attractions of the medium, and the only separation needed can be created with lighting. While only the front row is actually at the same level with the actors, the feeling of intimacy becomes contagious and spreads to the other two, four or five rows.

Every row, except the first one of course, should be raised about six to eight inches. With this arrangement every seat in the house will have equally good sightlines, an essential factor in any theatre, but doubly important in this medium; absolutely nothing must get in the way of the audience's seeing the performance. It is also advisable to provide for sufficient leg room. To make the audience comfortable and to create a true theatre atmosphere, regular theatre seats should be installed.

Tickets must be printed with section, row and seat numbers, just as they are in the conventional theatre. Although all seats are equally good, they must be reserved because theatregoers usually have preferences as to the section and row from which they want to see the play.

We have already observed that the number of aisleways varies considerably. It is conceivably possible to get along with only two; we have found three fairly suitable in Theatre '50, and Glenn Hughes and the Arena in New York use four. Norman Bel Geddes's plan includes eight aisleways, but I believe six would provide an ample variety of exits and entrances and would take care of the simultaneous appearance of a large crowd as well as facilitate seating late arrivals without disturbing the performance.

The length of the aisleways must be proportionate to the size of the playing area; they must never seem incongruously long or short. (An extremely long aisleway is particularly dangerous because it slows down the play whenever there is an entrance or an exit.)

Since the actors utilize the aisleways in darkness at the beginning and end of a scene, some theatres have supplied the edge of the carpeting with illuminated tape or paint.

Two of our aisleways have three steps leading to the exit, and we have found this elevation useful in many productions to suggest the beginning of a staircase, a balcony or another room. In a larger auditorium, it might be more advantageous to have portable units of steps, platforms and ramps which can be set up in different places, according to the requirements of the play.

The size and shape of the playing area must be in complete harmony with the room. Our auditorium in Dallas is in the shape of a keystone and, therefore, we have a trapezoid playing area. The tendency in designs for building theatres-in-the-round is towards the circular and elliptical shapes, and these are probably better because they offer a complete encircling of the stage by the audience. Since, however, in the next few years most new theatres will probably be organized without buildings constructed especially for them, they will adapt themselves to the shape of the space they find.

Our playing area at Theatre '50 is 24 feet by 20, which is an adequate size. Although it is possible to utilize a smaller area, ideally the stage should be at least 28 feet by 28, or 30 feet in diameter (again according to Bel Geddes's plan) if it is circular, because there would be sufficient space to avoid one of the shortcomings of all existent theatres-in-the-round, the spilling of light on the audience.

We have carpeted the playing area to the edge of the platform on which the second row of seats is located and the aisleways all the way to the exits; this is essential to avoid the noise that might be caused by an actor stepping off the carpet onto the floor which would prove very disturbing. A neutral color, either buff (which we use) or gray, seems advisable. If the budget permits it, the entire auditorium should be carpeted.

The height of the ceiling depends on the room, too. If you are building a theatre-in-the-round, the lighting setup should be determined before deciding on the height or type of ceiling. Both the Bel Geddes project and Glenn Hughes's Penthouse Theatre prefer a dome. Our ceiling is flat, but it has a dropped ceiling, approximately twelve feet high, which was originally built for indirect lighting and which we use for our house lights. Although it is preferable to have the lighting equipment invisible to the audience, if you are adapting a room for theatre-in-the-round, it may be impossible to mask all the lights. Several of the arena theatres now in existence make no attempt to hide the lamps, and this does not seem to distract the audience.

Lighting is important in any theatre, but it has several added functions in arena staging. It becomes the curtain which opens and closes a scene; it helps to suggest the physical setting of the play and to create the mood; it high lights and emphasizes the playing area as a focus. The stage becomes, as Kelley Yeaton has suggested in a very valuable article in *Players Magazine*, a pool of light, "a network of forces, a field of magnetic pulls, an opalescence of colors."

The width of our dropped ceiling is the same as that of the playing area; lengthwise it extends from the second row of seats to the back of the auditorium. Along this dropped ceiling and in a keystone shape, just outside the playing area, a board (1 by 6 inches) is lag-bolted into the ceiling, and the lights are mounted on this board. To make a canopy which partially masks the lights, metal sheeting one foot wide and six inches thick, bent at a right angle, is screwed into the thickness of the board and flush with the ceiling; this sheeting is also used to house the cable and as a teaser.

A smaller canopy, about 6 by 6 feet, is set up in exactly the same way in the center of the larger one, and lights are mounted on it too. The lights on both canopies are mounted one foot apart from each other. We use fifty 150-watt drama lights in bullet-type aluminum housing; these are the same type of louvred lights that are used in displays and offer lighting that is more diffused and less harsh. All the lights are mounted on universal swivel sockets, which means that they can be turned 180 degrees if necessary. They also take a permanent type of heat-resisting colored glass. Nine of these lights are located in the smaller canopy.

To cover the aisleways (entrances and exits included) three leicos of 500 watts each are placed in the smaller canopy; these are the standard type of ellipsoidal reflector with built-in metal shutters.

Four 500-watt Fresnel lights are located in the four corners of the larger canopy and two in the smaller one. They are used for special effects (motivating lights and blending).

We also have some additional equipment which is not permanently mounted but is utilized when a play requires it. This consists of two projection machines which, when needed, are placed above the dropped ceiling where the indirect lighting is located, and several small spots for pin-spotting or other special effects which can be mounted wherever the action demands additional lighting.

The lighting setup is visible to a portion of the audience, but there is no glare in their faces. There is, however, a reflection on the people in the front row (but no direct spill), which could be avoided only if space permitted moving the audience about six feet further back.

We use a regular portable switchboard of the type that most Broadway plays carry when touring. It has nine dimmer plates with the following distribution of strength: two have 1,800 watts, two 1,500 watts, and five 1,250 watts. We also built an additional pre-set board (and are now planning another one), containing six dimmers of 500 watts each which gives us a greater flexibility of lighting control. The house lights are controlled by a separate dimmer.

The switchboard is located in the control booth, from which the stage manager supervises the performance through a one-way vision window (which is not quite one foot square and should be considerably larger). The booth is also equipped with a second window, occasionally employed for the action of the play itself. For additional protection, the windows have flaps in back of them in case the lights in the control booth ever happen to be brighter than those in the auditorium.

The sound system, consisting of three turntables (two for regular speed records and one for long-playing speed), is in the same booth; two amplifiers are placed above the dropped ceiling, and from them emanate the music and sound effects for the play. A third amplifier is in the largest dressing room; a double-throw switch allows the stage manager to address the actors without any danger of being heard over the other amplifiers.

The control booth, which is the nerve center of the theatre, is behind and just above the last row of seats; it is separated from the auditorium proper by a plywood partition, which does not quite reach the floor, so that the actors can be heard by the stage manager.

A pilot-light system is utilized to signal actors. The stage manager has a board with three 7½-watt bulbs which correspond to the lights in the three exits and are wired in series.

In describing our lighting setup, I only want to show one way in which it can be done. Every imaginative designer will have a different approach, and the whole field of lighting an arena stage is still in the experimental phase. I think we should at all times bear in mind what Robert Edmond Jones said in his inspiring book, *The Dramatic Imagination*:

"The creative approach to the problem of stage lighting—the art, in other words, of knowing where to put light on the stage and where to take it away—is not a matter of textbooks and precepts. There are no arbitrary rules. There is only a goal and a promise. We have the mechanism with which to create this ideal, exalted, dramatic light in the theatre. Whether we can do so or not is a matter of temperament as well as of technique. The secret lies in our perception of light in the theatre as something alive.

"Does this mean that we are to carry images of poetry and vision and high passion in our minds while we are shouting out orders to electricians on ladders in light-rehearsals?

"Yes. This is what it means."

The theatre should be attractive and functional outside of the auditorium, too. There must be sufficient dressing-room space, of course, equipped with appropriate lighting, mirrors, lavatories, and, if at all possible, showers. Room is also needed for properties and furniture as well as for the sewing of costumes.

The foyer should be large enough to hold the entire audience in case of bad weather outside; a foyer surrounding the auditorium, such as the one the Penthouse Theatre in Seattle has, is ideal. As in any other theatre, provisions must be made for rest rooms, a cloakroom, a concession for the sale of refreshments and a heating and air-conditioning system. Theatre '50 has found it possible and interesting to offer its foyer to young artists for their exhibitions.

Choice of Plays

The list of plays which Theatre '50 has produced in its four seasons of existence will indicate that I do not believe theatre-in-the-round presents any limitations in the selection of scripts. Ideally, of course, we should have flexible theatres in which the method of production could be completely determined by the script. Any play, nevertheless, can be done in the round. The only problem lies in finding a good play which you want to do very badly.

Most of the plays of the past and the present are written for the proscenium stage, because it is the type of theatre we are best acquainted with; but if the proscenium arch had never been invented, could we not assume that every play has been written for theatre-in-the-round? The conventional theatre as we know it today removes the fourth wall; can we not remove the other three also and rely on the imagination of the spectator? We can because life does not go on just in front of us, but all around us.

The theatre-in-the-round encounters the same problems as the more conventional medium, but it can overcome them as well. Plays with large casts and many sets can be done in arena theatres, provided there is the imagination and willingness to put them on. The problems presented by swift scene changes, complicated scenery, or even simultaneous settings, can always be solved, frequently by simplifying them, as a description of our productions will show.

In the early history of theatre-in-the-round in America it was thought that the most suitable plays for theatre-in-the-round were drawing-room comedies, but since then, Shakespeare, Molière, Goldsmith, Ibsen and other classics have been successfully and beautifully presented in this medium, too.

Any style that can be essayed on the proscenium stage can be used in the round. A play can be done with a completely naturalistic approach, or it can be highly stylized. There is no restriction as to style; we can create realism as well as symbolism, expressionism or surrealism, depending on the requirements of the script.

Nor does it matter whether the play is light or serious; tragedies fare as well in this medium as comedies, farces or melodramas. I know of only one type of play which seems inadvisable to do in an intimate theatre: a drama in which the action contains so much horror that it may unnerve or even alienate an audience sitting at close range to the actors; but even such a play could be produced if the acting area were large enough to create a certain distance between the action and the spectator without destroying the intimacy.

I have already stated that my own belief and practice is to do only new plays and classics. My approach is to read scripts from whatever source they may arrive: playwrights, agents, friends who have discovered a fine play.

If the play is good and it is given a fine production, it is bound to look good from all directions. Plays do not have to be written or adapted for theatre-in-the-round; a director who knows his medium will use it to best advantage and therefore to the best advantage of the script.

Furniture and Properties

In arranging the floor plan for each play, the director distributes the furniture so that there will be as many playing areas as possible. The most obvious way to do this is to have an area in each one of the four corners, but as many variations can be found as there are in real rooms, gardens or other locations. With such a distribution, every section of the playhouse will at some time during the play have a good view of each actor. It is important to plan very carefully the direction in which each piece of furniture is going to face and to obtain a maximum of variety. The audience, however, must never be conscious of this arrangement; the whole set should give the impression of being "natural." No one area is given special emphasis since the focus has to be on the whole stage; this means that the placement and the quality of the furniture have to be well balanced. Rugs placed on the permanent carpet help to break up the stage into several acting areas.

All the furniture used in a theatre-in-the-round should be low enough so that it does not obstruct the view of any member of the audience. Chairs, armchairs, sofas and benches should have low backs or no backs at all, for the audience sees the actor from the back as well as from the front. Lamps, vases or other fairly tall decorations should never be placed on tables of regular height because they interfere with the sightlines. It is best to eliminate such objects, but if they are essential, they are set on very low tables, bookcases or chests.

Most arena stages are small and should not be crowded with unnecessary elements, but it is possible to create in this medium a set requiring a cluttered appearance; and if a piece of furniture or an ornament is needed solely to supply atmosphere, it must never be denied to the play.

Since virtually no scenery is employed, the furniture must be esthetically effective as well as functional. The actual beauty of a piece is of considerable importance, and so is its semblance to reality. If an exquisite rosewood table, for instance, is described in the dialogue of a play, it must not only be exquisite but also rosewood because the audience can see it at close range. This, of course, applies to properties as well.

Authenticity of furniture and props is observed according to the requirements of each play. Period furniture cannot be faked. Books must be precisely those referred to in the script; if the date of a newspaper or magazine is mentioned in the dialogue, that particular publication has to be found or else an exact replica must be prepared. If the audience does not notice these objects during the performance, it can do so at intermission time or when the play is over.

If the script calls for an eating scene, food is actually consumed by the actors. A certain amount of substitution is possible with liquids (tea or soda pops for alcoholic beverages, for instance), but a loaf of bread or a chicken leg or a slice of ham is almost impossible to fake.

Outdoor scenes are created with the use of garden furniture, a certain amount of shrubbery, a few plants, benches or other pieces suggesting an exterior. The ground is represented by the neutral-colored carpeting which remains bare. If a tree is needed and a small one will not do, the audience's imagination will be of great assistance. We have discovered that if the line of dialogue and the actor can suggest a piece of scenery or a prop, the audience will believe that it is there.

The same is true of pictures and mirrors which are supposed to be on a wall. The actor stares into space and, if he believes that he is examining a fine painting or looking at himself in a mirror, the audience will believe along with him. If, on the other hand, a picture or a mirror (or, for that matter, another prop) becomes an important factor in the play, it can be hung in the corner at the end of one of the aisleways or in some cases projected on the walls of this corner.

Doors and windows are placed off stage whenever possible and the drawing of draperies is suggested with lighting effects, but if any of these is essential to the action of the play, it may be placed in the aisleway.

A fender and a pair of andirons can constitute a fireplace. Logs and a light masked inside them can be added if the fireplace has to be functional, although this is rarely necessary. The audience will imagine the warmth and the smoke if the actors convey the feeling to them.

Sometimes a chandelier or some other property is hung from above in order to tie in the whole set and give it an added touch of atmosphere; this is especially helpful in stylized productions.

Authentic furniture and properties are usually borrowed or rented because the cost of purchasing them, especially in the case of period plays, would be prohibitive. Nor is it advisable to have the staff construct them, for it takes a long time and expert training to make good furniture. Items needed for nonrealistic productions, on the other hand, are built on the premises by the production crew.

Costumes and Make-Up

A theatre-in-the-round needs the services of a highly imaginative and skillful costume designer, for the costume creates a large portion of the atmosphere of the play. This applies especially to period plays.

The costume must be beautifully designed and perfectly executed. It has to be thoroughly authentic as to style, materials and the minutest detail because the proximity of the spectators enables them to examine it very closely. Faking is absolutely out of the question; it is impossible, for example, to substitute a cheap material when a glistening satin is required. In a play calling for richness and a lush quality, like Molière's *The Learned Ladies,* the exuberance of the costume is as important as the performance of the actor. The costume reflects the emotional impact of the play as well as its locale and its time.

In contemporary plays, clothes have to be carefully chosen, too, and must indicate the time and place of the action. If a character is to appear in a recently pressed tuxedo, it must be just that; a shabby dressing gown must show the years of wear.

As has already been pointed out, all our costumes are made on the premises and the actors can have their fittings without leaving the theatre, which is a highly satisfactory arrangement.

Period costumes are kept in storage, and ideally a theatre should have space for an ever-increasing wardrobe. With certain alterations costumes can be used again in plays of the same period, but preferably not during the same season. A major portion of the audience are subscribers and some of them are likely to recognize the costume as having been used in a previous production; this would destroy the illusion and the saving involved would not be worth it.

Because of the proximity of the audience, the use of make-up is very limited in theatre-in-the-round. Most actors and actresses employ pancake in preference to grease paint. Men can often play in this medium without any make-up at all, especially if they happen to have a good tan. Women normally apply little more than the usual street make-up.

An actor can be aged with lines and graying hair, but the make-up design and application have to be much more subtle than they are in the picture-frame theatre. It is preferable to dispense with wigs, except in period pieces or nonrealistic plays. The only rule to follow is that the audience must never be aware of theatrical make-up during the performance.

Directing and Acting

A good director in a picture-frame theatre is also a good director in theatre-in-the-round. The medium does not present any insurmountable problem; any director with experience and common sense can adjust to a different type of staging, and if he has imagination (which he should have in any kind of theatre!), he can direct plays as well in a theatre-in-the-round.

Because I believe this, many of the things I am going to say about directing in this chapter apply to any type of stage and only a few refer exclusively to theatre-in-the-round. I have found in going from one medium to the other—and I have often done this—that the basic principles and problems are the same: the approach to the play, the relationship to the actors and even the actual staging. "Treat the stage as a circle," wrote Arthur Hopkins in *Reference Point*, "not as a parallelogram. A well-staged play will look as convincing from the backstage wall as from the orchestra pit."

In addition to his own imagination, which he needs in any medium, the director must make use of the audience's imagination when he is working in theatre-in-the-round. The more he relies on the audience's capacity to imagine, the truer his results are likely to be. He must never be afraid that the audience will fail to respond when he invites them to use their intelligence. Everybody has imagination; it is up to the director to stimulate it.

The director's first job in a resident professional theatre, whether it utilizes central staging or not, is the preparation of the entire season. It is preferable to allow two or three months' time for this purpose so that all the new plays can be chosen (a director reads new plays all the time, and some selections will have been made before the preceding season is over), and a number of classics read or re-read before deciding on these.

A season has to be well balanced. It stands to reason that it would be very taxing to do one costume play after another; an attempt should be made, therefore, to follow a period drama with a contemporary play, or at least one in which the costumes will not be as difficult (unless the theatre already has the costumes in its wardrobe). The audience will also appreciate a certain amount of variety in this regard.

For a theatre with a small staff and company, it is wise to alternate large-cast plays with smaller ones, since the former will require the services of the production assistants as well as all the other actors.

Besides fitting into the season, each play must be like a friend to the director; a play, like a person, has an individuality of its own, and this individuality must have a special appeal to the director. He must love the play and want very much to do it. And he must establish an absolute rule for himself: that he will not do a play he does not want to direct. Let us hope that the wants of the director will always lead to an improvement of standards.

When you read a play after having had a certain amount of experience in the theatre, there are certain elements you look for automatically. Are the story and characters believable? Does the play have a unifying idea or theme or impact? Is this unifying element dramatized in the action of the play? Is it universal enough; that is, does it make you care? Does it have a sufficiently powerful or exciting conflict? Is there consistent and logical character motivation? Does the play have an inner organization of its own so that it will be intelligible to the audience and mean something to them?

But I repeat that all these questions become automatic. I do not believe you can apply any of them as a measuring stick to a work of art. It all adds up to one question which presupposes that you have the adequate preparation and taste: do you like the play enough to do it?

Once the director has chosen the play, he must plan to spend enough time with it to understand it thoroughly, to know exactly what the author intended to do in each scene, in each act. This means, of course, that the director must confer with the author and reach an agreement about the interpretation of the play as well as straighten out any special problems the script may present.

With a three-week rehearsal period, it is better to

have all the re-writing done before rehearsals begin. As a rule, I do not let myself fall in love with a script unless it is almost in condition to be produced. It is unwise to schedule a play for production during the forthcoming season if you are not sure that it will be ready. When the play is read by the actors and when it is on its feet, both the director and the author may want certain revisions, but these are usually minor and can easily be made during the rehearsal period.

For this reason, and also because it is mutually beneficent to the playwright and the director and actors, the author should be available when needed during all rehearsals and for the run of the play. If his other occupations do not permit this, he should at least be at the theatre for the last rehearsals and the opening night. Playwrights develop and improve with the productions they get.

When the author and the director feel the need to discuss the play during the rehearsal period, they should do so outside the theatre and in the absence of the actors. Actors may frequently have valuable suggestions for the improvement of the script, but they should make them to the director, who, if he considers them pertinent, will pass them on to the author. In the same way, any criticism the playwright has of the actors should be given to the director.

The director must also be able to understand the actor and his problems and give the actor an opportunity to express himself. It is wonderful if the director can make his company fall in love with the plays selected for the season; strong enthusiasm is contagious, and the director should not hesitate to communicate to the actors his convictions about a script.

From a practical point of view, it would be best to cast all the plays before the season begins and assign each actor the parts he is to play during the forthcoming thirty or forty weeks. There are, however, two flaws in this procedure. The director is not completely sure of the potentialities of the actor (this refers primarily to new members of the company) until the middle of the season; and secondly, the actor might develop a special affection for one of the many roles he has to portray and give most of his concentration to that part.

For the most part, I do not cast a play until it is about to go into rehearsal, although I may have distributed certain parts in my own mind. Before the first reading of a script, every member of the company is given a copy; at this point it is highly advisable to tell the actor what part he is to play. If, however, the director is not quite sure yet, he can ask the actor to read a certain part with the understanding that he may not be cast in it. This must be done very tactfully, lest the actor be terribly disappointed if he does not get the part he first read.

I think that a director can obtain the best results from any actor if he pulls them out of the actor himself.

Any method which will work is acceptable, but I do not believe it is creative to show an actor how to deliver a line or perform a piece of business, unless the director finds that this is the only way to make the actor aware of the truth. There is no magic in the theatre if every actor is imitating the director. Actors must be taught to love the process of thinking. They, too, have imagination, and it is up to the director to make them use it.

Before rehearsals start, the director confers with the technical director and the costume designer about the production scheme, which includes the floor plan, the lighting, sound and musical effects, furniture, costumes and props.

The actual rehearsal procedure varies with the play. Certain scripts should be read by the actors a number of times before being blocked out; others should be placed on their feet as soon as humanly possible. With a short rehearsal schedule, it is wise to start blocking the play early, memorizing the lines and working out fine points of characterization and stage business later.

Our rehearsal period consists of three weeks, but during this time the company is playing six evening performances and two matinees every week. Under such circumstances, it would be desirable to have four weeks, and this is feasible if each play can have that long a run. Ideally, too, there should be one week of rehearsals in full costume and with all props, especially in the case of a period play in which the actors need time to become accustomed to the costume and to learn to use it functionally and gracefully.

No one but the staff, the actors and the author can be admitted to a rehearsal. This is an ironclad rule in our theatre, and I think an important one. The presence of one outsider frequently forces the actor to attempt a performance (for which he is not yet ready) and ruins the rehearsal. Fear of criticism and desire for commendation inevitably appear if a stranger is in the house. We have a serious job to get done in the theatre and must not be disturbed by visitors during working hours.

While I believe that the director should have a thorough knowledge of the play and a definite interpretation, everything cannot be taken care of in advance planning. There is a need for more experimentation in directing if we are to get away from the obvious, and the preparation of a detailed blueprint has a tendency to enslave you with its limitations. A director has to remain flexible, so that if the script acquires new aspects when put on its feet, he can take advantage of them and even investigate them further.

Theatre-in-the-round, although it has a rich history behind it, is such a new medium today that it calls for all the experimentation the director can give it. This applies to lighting, sound and music as well as to directorial approaches. Open-mindedness will always help to develop a theatre, to meet challenges, to find new ways of solving problems.

A play on an arena stage has to look good from all directions. The best way to plan the composition is to take a bird's-eye view, to imagine yourself looking at the production from the ceiling or the dome. In the proscenium theatre the audience sees the play from one direction only; the play is observed as a picture. The play becomes more like a sculpture in theatres-in-the-round; in other words, it acquires new dimensions. It means that the necessities are fourfold. It also means that the potentialities of exciting design are greater.

Sightlines from every portion of the house have to be borne constantly in mind, although this becomes an automatic process for a director who has worked any length of time in this medium. You can move from one section of the theatre to another during a rehearsal, but after a while, you will find that this is only a checking system because the solving of sightline problems has become a part of your entire production scheme.

An actor's back can be as effective and dramatic as his face; it is only a matter of using the whole body. A hand or the back of a head can convey to the audience as much as a facial expression, and good actors are well aware of that on the proscenium stage, too. At one point in our production of *The Importance of Being Earnest*, Lady Bracknell's reaction to Jack Worthing was expressed by a false smile; since only a portion of the audience witnessed this smile, the actress accompanied it with a bounce of her bustle, which gave the same effect to the remainder of the house. The resulting laugh was the same throughout the theatre.

Actors should never be moved merely to vary their position in relation to the audience. A movement has to have as much motivation as it does in any other type of theatre. On the other hand, if the movement can be motivated, it is good to know that theatre-in-the-round can take more movement than the picture-frame stage because it does not detract from the focus, which is your entire playing area.

The audience must never feel that an actor is moving around for their benefit, or the believability of the performance is destroyed.

I have coined the term "making the rounds" as applied to an actor showing his face to all sections of the house while he remains in the same area. For instance, if he has a long telephone conversation on stage, he can find motivation to turn in all directions during the scene. The same applies to a character who is addressing others sitting around him. A maximum of variations can be found without resorting to any artificial movements.

Focus is obtained very easily in theatre-in-the-round since the whole playing area is so close to the audience. The focal point is different for the various sections of the audience, but the emotional effect is the same for everybody. In fact, it is impossible not to get focus in central staging if the mood and the tempo of the play are correct.

Emphatic focus can be given to an actor by putting him on his feet, but such a movement must have its proper motivation in the action of the play.

If two people are seated and have a long conversation scene, it is handled in the same way as on the proscenium stage except that every section of the house is getting a different view. The director must never feel that it is imperative to break up the scene, for the focus is divided between the actor who is talking and the actor who is reacting to the words; and a portion of the audience, which sees the profiles of both actors, will receive an added impact from the scene.

There is an auditory as well as a visual focus in theatre-in-the-round. Hearing the actor whose face is turned away can create a focal point in itself, although in most cases the audience hears one person and sees another's face simultaneously.

Another reason why focus is no problem in this medium is that there are no weak playing areas, no up- or downstage. The aisleways and the corners are the only relatively weak spots because one fourth of the audience usually have to crane their necks to see them. The proximity of the spectator keeps from rendering them totally weak, but these areas should be used only when the play calls for a piece of scenery or a prop which cannot possibly be placed in the central space. Sometimes a prop can be projected on the wall of one of the corners. This method should be used only if the object is essential to the play. We have tried to use projections in order to suggest atmosphere or an off-stage locale, but have found that it only detracts from the focus.

Every detail of expression and bodily movement is significant in theatre-in-the-round. The flicker of an eye-lash, the removal of a glove, the slightest motion of a foot produce as strong an effect as a bigger movement. Everything which happens to the actor while on stage is seen by the audience and, therefore, every one of those things must count.

Very little has been done as yet to emphasize these details and stress a focal point through the use of lighting effects. It is conceivable, however, that in a certain scene two pin spots will show the audience nothing but the face of an actor and his hand, or the restless tapping of one actor's foot and the triumphant expression on another's face. This is only one small example of what can be eventually achieved with lights in this medium.

In most of our productions the lights go up and down at the beginning and end of a scene with the accompaniment of music. The actual co-ordination of the two elements depends largely upon the play; sometimes it is possible to let the music continue after the lights have gone up in order to help create the mood. Music can also be played during a scene for atmospheric effect if the tone of the play permits it. The movies have been aware of the emotional power of music in the background, and there is no reason why the theatre cannot use it too.

Dancing scenes or choreographic movement in a stylized production have proved so effective in this medium that I would like to do a dance-drama-in-the-round before long. Several summer stock companies have already discovered the possibility of presenting musical comedies and operettas on arena stages.

To the actor, theatre-in-the-round offers excellent training in honesty and concentration, for here no faking is possible; but I believe that a good actor on the proscenium stage is a good actor in any medium, and all he needs to do is to adapt himself to a few different requirements, which have already been discussed in connection with directing.

The actor is still giving a performance. Intimacy does not take the theatrics out of the theatre. This is especially important regarding projection. It is true that the actor is facing half the audience and that they are very close to him, but his voice must also reach the people to whom his back is turned. A few performances on an arena stage enable most actors to reach a golden mean of vocal projection, which makes them heard by one portion of the audience without having to shout into the ears of the other portion.

George Mitchell, who was a member of our acting company, wrote an article entitled "Actor-in-the-Round" in the New York *Times*, in which he said: "Consider the plight of the actor who is a stranger to these surroundings (the pun is intended). There is no scenery to turn to in embarrassing moments, no wings to escape into, no friendly prompter's voice, no glaring, shielding footlights, no curtain . . . No nothing but a circular sea of leering, peering faces often closer to you than the nearest actor's.

"Standing under the glare of the overhead lights on that first unforgettable entrance, I felt like a naked unanesthetized victim about to undergo a public major operation. I said my opening lines automatically and remembered to move over and sit on the divan in the dead center of the stage. My hands felt enormous, swollen, awkward beyond belief. My frozen smile began to twitch. When another actor leaned over me, I stared intently at him, trying to blot out the mass of eager, bulbous faces right behind him. When he circled around me, my eyes followed him, and those bleary faces swam by in the reverse direction."

But, then, George Mitchell talks about the virtues of the medium when the actor becomes accustomed to it: ". . . there is great freedom of movement, a complete and final break from the classic face-front technique; you learn to act with your back, your sides, your obliques. You can neither upstage nor be upstaged. And far better try lying to your own mother than attempt to give a false performance before the searching eyes of such a proximate audience." He ends his article with this statement: "And the actor, as though seeing himself under a microscope, improves his technique with many refinements."

There are a few technical points to be added, although I believe that most of them will be clarified in the discussion of each one of our productions in the following chapter.

In scenes which require the simultaneous entrance or exit of a crowd, the aisleways must be left completely free of furniture and props; in other words, nothing must block the entrances.

Getting actors on and off the stage has to be thoroughly rehearsed since this will take place in the darkness at the beginning and end of scenes; even if illuminated tape or paint is used, the actor should know exactly where he is going. In our theatre this is somewhat facilitated by the handrails of the stairs leading to the seats.

When the actors are on the dark stage, they give the stage manager a signal so that he can bring the lights up. This signal must be given by the last actor to appear on the stage, which means that the sequence in which the actors take their places has to be carefully arranged. It is better to make the signal a part of the play. For instance, there is a tap on the table, the lights go up, there is another tap as the audience sees that the character is in a tavern and calling for a waiter. Or a play opens with a woman who is angrily beating her newspaper against a chair; if she starts this action a second before the lights go up, it will serve as a signal. Once we used a sneeze as a signal because the character had to go on sneezing as the play started, but this is dangerous because a member of the audience might sneeze, too, and give the stage manager the wrong cue.

We have produced twenty-nine plays in our four seasons, and the occasion for prompting has never arisen. Although we go on the supposition that prompting will not be necessary, the book is kept at all times either by the stage manager or by one of his assistants. Actors do get into trouble with their lines, but they prefer to get themselves out of it. As a last resort, an actor could be prompted, but the audience would inevitably hear it.

If a musical instrument is played on the stage, the actor must learn to use it, and I have found that it is possible to do so even if the actor is not a musician. Faking the playing of a violin or an accordion and bringing the music over the loudspeaker would create a ludicrous effect in an intimate theatre and would destroy the illusion for the audience. This applies only to realistic productions, however; when you are stylizing, such faking can be an added source of humor.

Cards have to be carefully stacked for a poker or

gin-rummy game, and whatever the game is the actor must learn to play it correctly because the audience is watching every card and playing along with him. No matter how obscure the game might be, someone in the house is likely to know it.

Sword play has to be staged very carefully in theatre-in-the-round. There is the danger of actually hurting somebody, and there is the possibility of frightening the audience. Both of these have to be taken into account in planning any scene involving the use of swords. Up until last season, we tried to make the swords very short, keep them out of the audience's way and avoid fighting on the stage; but in our production of *Romeo and Juliet* a fight scene had to take place, and the swords had to be authentic. We found that with very careful rehearsing of every minute detail of the fighting, it was possible to do it without alarming the public.

Gunshots also tend to frighten an audience, and we have refrained from firing a gun on stage; this has been successfully accomplished, however, in other arena theatres and needs further experimentation with the accompanying sound effects.

The Audience

The audience comes into a theatre-in-the-round, as it does into any other playhouse, to see a good play well performed. They come to laugh and to cry, to be entertained and to be enlightened, to think and to live vicariously through interesting and exciting experiences. When our theatre was being organized, John Lineaweaver, a young writer then stationed in Dallas, wrote me about the expectations of the audience: "We want you to attract and nourish a share of sanity, talent and craftsmanship, and thereby make for us a living thing. In a manner of speaking, we want you to write a love letter to this aching world."

The theatre owes the audience a certain magic. There is a hush and an excitement in a picture-frame theatre when the house lights are dimmed, the footlights go on and the curtain is about to rise. The same kind of glamour and magic can be created when lights and music are used for a curtain, provided that what the audience sees and hears afterwards is of high quality.

There is no doubt that the first time a spectator walks into a theatre-in-the-round he has to adjust himself to a new medium. John Mason Brown, reporting a visit to our theatre in *The Saturday Review of Literature*, said that before the performance started, "I had my doubts as to what I was about to see. The arrangement both of the auditorium and the stage smacked suspiciously of a stunt. In one corner of the acting area, within breathing distance from me to be exact, were a few chairs and a table to indicate a room. At the opposite corner were a few more chairs and a sofa to suggest a room in another house. Between them was a small arch, covered with gray material, which I soon learned was to do valiant duty as a hill.

"Although curious about what I was in for, I cannot pretend I was happy. . . . Somehow, too," he adds, "I distrusted the whole setup. It smacked of artyness, which in itself can be a plague.

"But I was wrong. Totally, hopelessly, and happily wrong." And he goes on to say that the ". . . experiment with illusion proved for me at least to open unsuspected windows wide on what can be stuffy and is seldom ventilated in theatre practice."

John Mason Brown was also interested in the fact that "performers were merged to a degree not even guessed at in our customary auditoriums. More than being spectators, playgoers had for once come close to being participants. Moreover, I felt the joys of that stimulating pleasure which the theatre seldom grants to us who sit out front. I mean the pleasure which comes from having the imagination called upon to do its contributive work instead of being dismissed from active duty."

On a first visit to an arena theatre, spectators in the front row may feel a little stiff, but soon they are demanding to be seated nowhere else in the house. They may also be aware of the faces across the room from them, but if the play is engrossing enough this awareness disappears, or at least it ceases to be a disturbing factor. Seeing each other's faces may be an advantage in the case of very humorous scenes because the laughter becomes visual as well as auditory and is more contagious.

The simplicity of the medium is refreshing. In his weekly column in *The New York Times Book Review,* J. Donald Adams wrote after witnessing a performance-in-the-round: "It seems to me that theatre-in-the-round can have a special appeal in our period, which is one that has been surfeited with spectacle and starved of participation. You cannot realize, until you have seen a good play well performed in this intimate manner, how incidental the stage set actually is. The modern theatre has overemphasized its role, even to the point of sometimes making it an encumbrance—as well as an expense. The motion picture has gorged itself on spectacle, and there are times at a big football game when the actual play seems incidental."

Brooks Atkinson, in one of his articles in *The New York Times,* said that arena style ". . . has two incomparable virtues: it awakens a theatregoer's imagination, which should be a primary function of theatre, and its fundamental magic of appealing to and stimulating the ear more than the eye. When it is thus reduced to its primary qualities of literature and acting without the impedimenta of an opulent production, the theatre is wonderfully fresh, social and enriching."

I have a great deal of reverence for visual beauty, and I believe that theatre-in the round offers a new territory for the imagination of our designers, not in terms of actual scenery, but of color, design, ornament. The theatre consists of the script plus the visual element, and this does not mean that the latter has to be overburdened with great structures.

Elsewhere in the above-mentioned article, Mr. Atkinson writes: "The audience has a complete sense of participation; it is drawn intimately into the spirit of the play and acting. The performance goes fast; the response is immediate and thorough."

In any theatre, when the curtain rises, the audience is being transported to a different world. Theatre-in-the-round provides this feeling, and at the same time makes the audience a part of this different, new, imaginary yet very real world.

CHAPTER FIVE

Log of Plays Produced by Theatre '50

Since our opening in 1947, we have had four seasons and produced twenty-nine plays. Eighteen of them have been new scripts, and eleven classics; fifteen have been serious plays and fourteen comedies or farces.

The purpose of this log, in addition to giving a brief description of the play, is to point out why each script was chosen and some of the special problems which occurred in production.

First Season

FARTHER OFF FROM HEAVEN, *by William Inge.*

This was the first professional production for William Inge, who was to write *Come Back Little Sheba,* produced by the Theatre Guild in 1950.

A realistic play, set in a small town in Kansas in the early 1920's, *Farther Off From Heaven* showed that the author had a genuine compassion for the family around which the drama is built. With heart-warming simplicity he presented their problems, their frustrations and their joys. Andrew Campbell, the father, is a traveling shoe salesman, and the few days he spends at home are not always the happiest because somehow the problems always creep to the surface at this time. His wife, Sarah, struggles valiantly to keep the home going, no matter how bad the economic and personal hardships tend to become.

The children have their agonies too. The teen-aged Irene is a homely little girl who has a broken tooth to boot. When she finally manages to have a date, the empty space in her mouth is covered with paraffin, but her father is unwilling to pay for the $19.50 party dress. Her younger brother, Sonny, prefers collecting pictures of 1920 movie stars to playing football and finds himself cried out a "sissy" by the school bullies.

The story is pathetic, yet it has its comic aspects. Mrs. Campbell's sister, who chatters incessantly, her long-suffering husband, and the young blade who takes Irene out on a date are characters secondary to the plot, but they enhance the atmosphere of the play.

The mention of movie stars of the period (Sonny wants to see Pola Negri's first picture), the recital of an Edgar Guest poem, the hand-crank phonograph help to set the period of the play. Add to this the very ordinary furniture and costuming which would have a feel of the 'twenties, and the picture is complete.

Since we did not have any children in the company, the little girl was played by one of our actresses who looked young enough for the part, and for Sonny we were fortunate to find a local boy who had experience on the professional stage.

The phonograph, with records of the period, was actually played on stage. The script called for the beginning of a staircase which we represented with the three steps at the end of one of our aisleways.

HOW NOW, HECATE, *by Martyn Coleman.*

An English farce, set in the converted barn of a large estate, this play was classified by John Rosenfield in his review as "a comedy in the blithe spirit of Noel Coward's most recent spoofing on supernaturalism."

The plot revolves around a scholarly writer, an unscrupulous actress who is after him, and a spinsterish sorceress who appears every seven years wherever two planets cojoin on the night of a full moon. Before the actress is converted into a suitable wife for the hero, innumerable tricks occur on the stage. This presented a challenge for theatre-in-the-round and proved that we could handle as much stage trickery in this medium as on the proscenium stage.

Miss Ogilvie prepares her magic brew in a cauldron which boils on the logs of the fireplace. We obtained some spooky effects by placing multi-colored lights between the logs. In this case we did not feel it would be advisable to let the audience imagine the smoke (the story itself made sufficient demands on their imagination!), and we used dry ice to make smoke appear.

At one point in the play Miss Ogilvie turns the actress into a cat. Now, it is possible to use animals in theatre-in-the-round, but they will drive you insane. The first cat we engaged got her notice before long because she was a bit too temperamental; the second one, who became known to us as Hecate, was a pretty good trouper. But while the cat had rehearsed the play, she had never heard applause at the end of a scene; and so, on opening night, as the lights went down and the audience clapped, Hecate became very frightened and clawed the actress who was holding her. This made the actress lose her way in the dark, and she landed in the lap of a gentleman on the front row, who realized her predicament and helped her to the exit.

To reveal Hecate as the missing actress, the cat had to eat a whole bowl of caviar (the actress's favorite dish). The cat had no objections to this delicacy, but since we found it would prove rather expensive, we provided her with crushed sardines instead.

The time of the play is September, and there is a thunderstorm in the midst of the eery proceedings; we supplied the sound effects with a thundersheet off stage.

HEDDA GABLER, *by Henrik Ibsen.*

Hedda was the first classic to be done by Theatre '50 and proved that Ibsen's work could be brought out very well in intimate style. Enthusiastically, John Rosenfield opened his review with this statement: "Theatre-'47-in-the-round may be just the milieu *Hedda Gabler* has needed for a half century," and later in the review he explained: "Never before had we found *Hedda* so natural and so human, a story of persons instead of a saga of personages. To the surface came the Ibsen humor; not hearty fun, to be sure, but humor, nevertheless, or rather mordant wit. The audience discovered it could laugh with Ibsen at Professor Tesman's naïveté, at Hedda's outrageous perverseness . . . at Judge Brack's cynical gallantries."

Hedda has a passionate desire to find great beauty in life, but she is destroyed by her fear of scandal, her concern with other people's opinion and, above all, by her lack of interest in anything her environment can provide. The source of her downfall is her background—wealthy, arrogant, selfish and snobbish. There is a potential of stature in Hedda, but she does not know how to cope with life. And Ibsen presents the shadow of death very early in the play, for Aunt Rina Tesman is doomed in the first act.

There are many avenues to explore. Hedda has married George Tesman on the spur of the moment, possibly because he bought a house she had casually mentioned to make conversation, and now she is afraid that marriage and ensuing motherhood may deprive her of her individuality. She is disgusted with her husband's affection; intimacy with him seems hateful to her. But she once had an interest—Eilert Lovborg, a writer of true genius—and the appearance of Mrs. Elvsted, who is now in love with Eilert, re-awakens Hedda's concern with him. Here is her opportunity to mold a human destiny, the one thing which will elevate her above her fellow men. She observes Mrs. Elvsted and Lovborg, discovers that they have established between them a close intellectual bond, and decides to destroy both the bond and Eilert. She pursues her objective relentlessly until she places one of her father's pistols in Lovborg's hand and tells him to do it "beautifully."

But she is trapped by Judge Brack, a former suitor who is not attracted by the idea of matrimony, because he knows she has given the gun to Eilert. When she finds out that Eilert has committed suicide but not at all "beautifully," and that his manuscript (which she has burned) can be restored by Mrs. Elvsted with the painstaking co-operation of George Tesman, she is at her wit's end. Cornered by Brack and completely in his power, she decides to put an end to her life, and does do it "beautifully." She had hoped to influence Tesman's life as well as Eilert's by destroying the manuscript, but ironically it is her husband who will make Eilert's memory live, and it is Mrs. Elvsted who may be able to mold even Tesman's destiny!

The climactic moment of the play is the third-act curtain when Hedda throws the manuscript into the fire. ("Now I am burning your child, Thea! Burning it, curly-locks! Your child and Eilert Lovborg's. I am burning—I am burning your child.") We used an old-fashioned stove with a light in it. Part of the audience could see the fire in the stove; the others saw the light reflected on Hedda's face.

The suicide took place off stage, which eliminated the gunshot within close range of the audience; I also found it more effective not to let the audience see Hedda after she is dead.

The period of the play (1890's) was depicted by the costumes and hair-dos as well as by the furniture and props. The set is divided into a living room and an adjoining music room. We had the living room take up most of the playing area, and two low bookcase pieces separated it from the music room which started near one of the aisleways. The piano had to be placed off stage because a grand piano would have occupied too much space, and an upright piano, besides being wrong for the period, would have proved too high to allow for good sightlines.

SUMMER AND SMOKE, *by Tennessee Williams.*

Here was an example of a playwright who had had a Broadway production, was on the verge of another one, yet wanted a play of his to be done by a resident professional theatre. *Summer and Smoke* is a play combining delicate poetry and great human passions; it has many of the wonderful qualities that made me fall in love with *The Glass Menagerie,* but like every true work of art, it has a life of its own.

To introduce the play Williams uses a quote from Rainer Maria Rilke:

> "Who, if I were to cry out, would hear me among the angelic order?"

And from this through the twelve scenes of *Summer and Smoke* every moment is filled with character-revealing detail, with theatricality in the best sense of the word, with the kind of poetry that the contemporary theatre has been starved for.

The play is in two moods, reflected by the time of the year. Williams has labeled part one a summer; part two, a winter. And in his prefatory notes to the play, the author speaks of the sky:

"There must be a great expanse of sky so that the entire action of the play takes place against it. This is true of interior as well as exterior scenes. But in fact there are no really interior scenes, for the walls are omitted or just barely suggested by certain necessary fragments such as might be needed to hang a picture or to contain a doorframe.

"During the day scenes the sky should be a pure and intense blue (like the sky of Italy as it is so faithfully represented in the religious paintings of the Renaissance), and costumes should be selected to form dramatic color contrasts to this intense blue which the figures stand against. (Color harmonies and other visual effects are tremendously important.)

"In the night scenes, the more familiar constellations, such as Orion and the Great Bear and the Pleiades, are clearly projected on the night sky, and above them, splashed across the top of the cyclorama, is the nebulous radiance of the Milky Way. Fleecy cloud forms may also be projected on this cyclorama and made to drift across it."

It was impossible to follow all of the playwright's suggestions in theatre-in-the-round, but we could and did take the cue for our lighting from his words. Another one of his suggestions we were able to carry out more satisfactorily: "Everything possible should be done to give an unbroken fluid quality to the sequence of scenes."

The play calls for four sets: the fountain, the rectory interior, the doctor's office and the arbor at Moonlake Casino. The first three are used simultaneously and were, therefore, on stage throughout the play. The fountain was extremely low, and the angel on it very small. Nor was it necessary to make the fountain practical; when the children bend over to take a drink, they convince the audience that the water is there. The interiors were suggested with a minimum of furniture, and the action shifted from one area to another with the use of lights and music.

For the fourth set—the Casino scene—we used the largest area which had remained clear of furniture (that is, between two of the already established sets) and lighted this empty spot. As the lights went up, a waiter appeared whistling as he carried a small table onto the stage. In a second he returned with a couple of chairs and walked off again, still whistling. Presently Alma and John, the protagonists of the play, made their entrance, called the waiter and the scene began.

The Fourth-of-July-fireworks scene requires almost a big production number, but it was managed effectively and simply by using pop sounds over the loudspeaker system and lighting the actors' faces, as they looked, up with intermittent red lights.

We used the same two actors who had played the children in *Farther Off From Heaven* to portray Alma and John in the prologue, which takes place at the turn of the century.

I believe *Summer and Smoke* contains more light, sound and music cues than any play I know of, and we found it possible to handle them all in a theatre-in-the-round production.

Needless to say, it is a great incentive for the staff and company of a theatre to be working on a fine play by one of the outstanding contemporary playwrights in the entire world. Every one of our productions is considered a landmark for us, but this sensitive drama about the quest of the spirit and the flesh and their battle as they meet and part and meet again was a moment of distinction in our first season.

THIRD COUSIN, *by Vera Mathews.*

To close the brief first season, I chose a very light farce which should—and did—provide the audience with a great deal of laughter.

The title of the play refers to a distant relative of Carrie Butterworth's, a college professor's widowed mother, who quite suddenly becomes clairvoyant. She is endowed with this new mystic power by her third cousin, who, although dead these past five years, has chosen to converse with Carrie.

With a slight story, but much farcical inventiveness, the play moves swiftly from one amusing situation to the next and has really delightful moments.

Since the script called for two settings—a living room and the professor's book-lined study—we outlined a small area with low bookcases, and this became the study. Placing different rugs in the two rooms helped to draw a dividing line.

Second Season

THE MASTER BUILDER, *by Henrik Ibsen.*

Hedda Gabler had shown us that Ibsen's plays fitted beautifully into our medium, so it seemed logical to start the second season with another one of his great plays, the story of architect Halvard Solness.

Solness is the symbol of the successful artist who has missed happiness in life and who, at the pinnacle of his career, begins to disintegrate because he is afraid that he will never again be able to build churches and climb the steeples to place upon them the wreaths of achievement. The younger generation, represented by a talented and progressive young man who works in his office, is on the verge of replacing him, but Solness is not yet prepared to give up.

Another aspect of the new generation is portrayed by the youthful Hilda Wangel, who had seen Solness place the last wreath on a steeple ten years earlier and comes to look him up. She is a carefree spirit who seeks communion with this genius she has set on a pedestal. At her insistence, he undertakes to climb to the heights once again, and although he falls and is killed, we feel that he has recaptured his freedom from fear and frustration.

Written only a year and a half after *Hedda,* this play indicates more of a tendency on Ibsen's part to fill his play with symbols and to add mysticism to the realistic drama.

Ibsen also created one of his most tragic characters in the figure of Aline Solness, the architect's wife, who bemoans the loss of her whole environment in the fire which burned down her old house. Her own children died in this fire and thereby she lost the function and mission she had in life, building the souls of little children. She goes on living because it is her "duty" and for no other reason.

Although the script calls for three settings—two interiors and one exterior—we found it both feasible and advisable to combine the two interiors into one, which was Halvard Solness's study and office. This did not necessitate any changes whatsoever in the play. Between acts two and three, the set was completely changed, and the veranda scene was furnished with iron garden chairs and benches as well as a few low urns with greenery.

A mirror in which the women looked at themselves to adjust their hats was imagined on the wall and so were the numerous books which Hilda admires in Solness's study.

Towards the end of the play, Hilda has to watch the architect climbing to a great height, an action he, of course, performs outside of the audience's range of vision. This effect has to be achieved by the actress playing Hilda, and it is a problem which is encountered on the proscenium stage as well—Hilda has to look off stage and make the audience believe that she watches Solness's progress.

A BILL OF THREE ONE-ACT PLAYS, *by Tennessee Williams.*

There is no doubt that in the last decade the professional theatre in this country has not been able to make a success of an evening of one-act plays. Perhaps the audience is looking for a unity and an organization which it

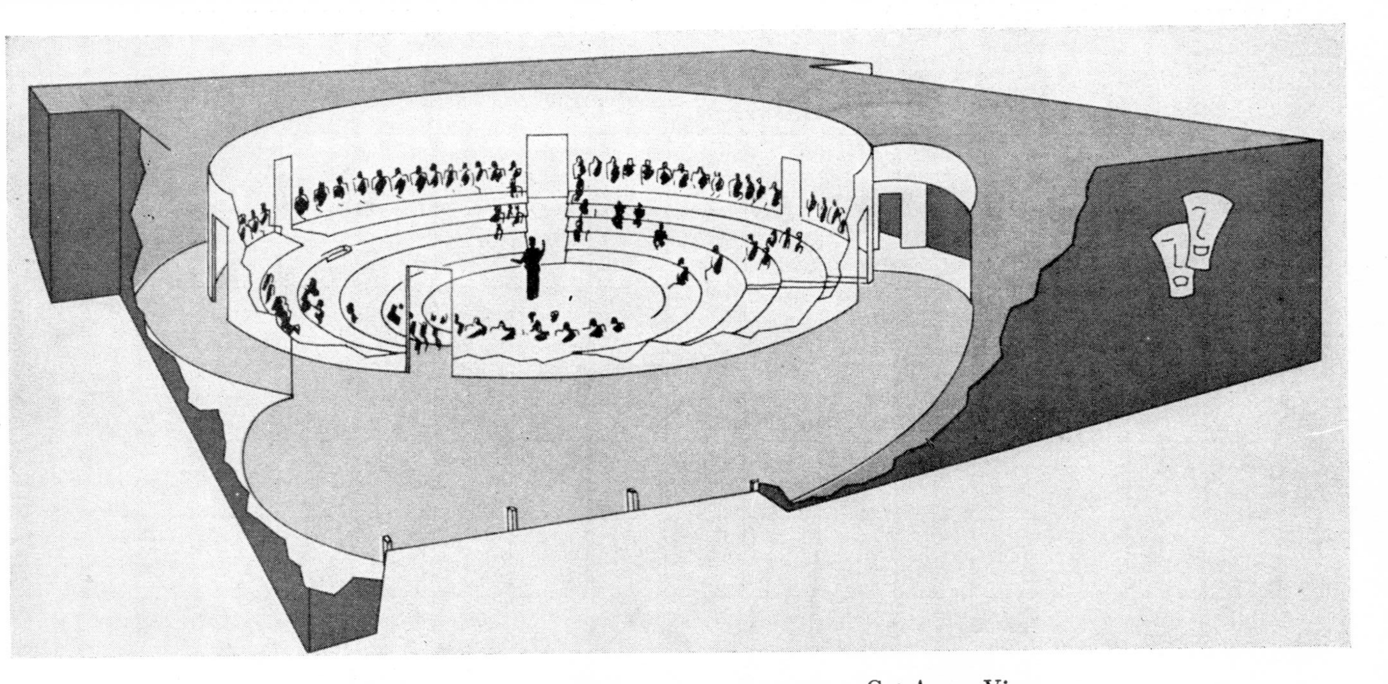

THE PLAYHOUSE THEATRE OF HOUSTON, TEXAS: Cut-Away View

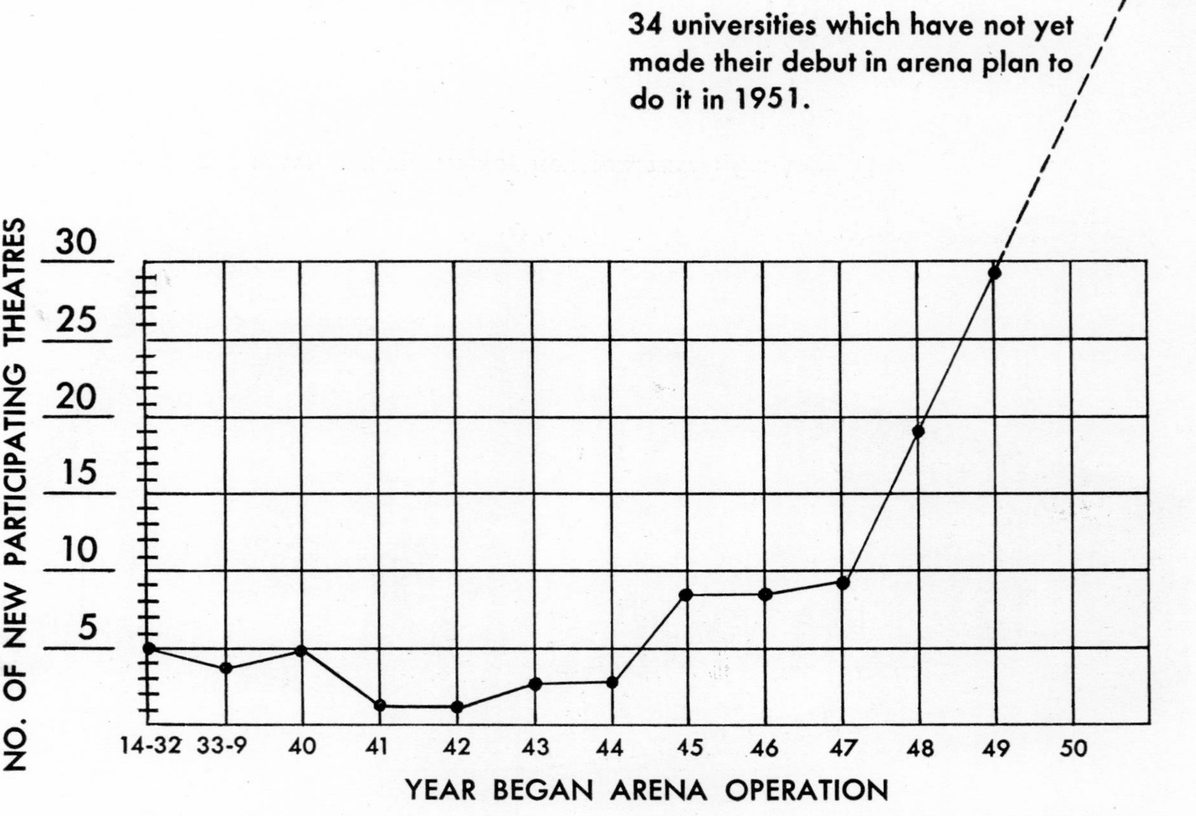

The Growth of THEATRE-IN-THE-ROUND Staging in the United States (*Graph prepared by Charles H. Gray,*

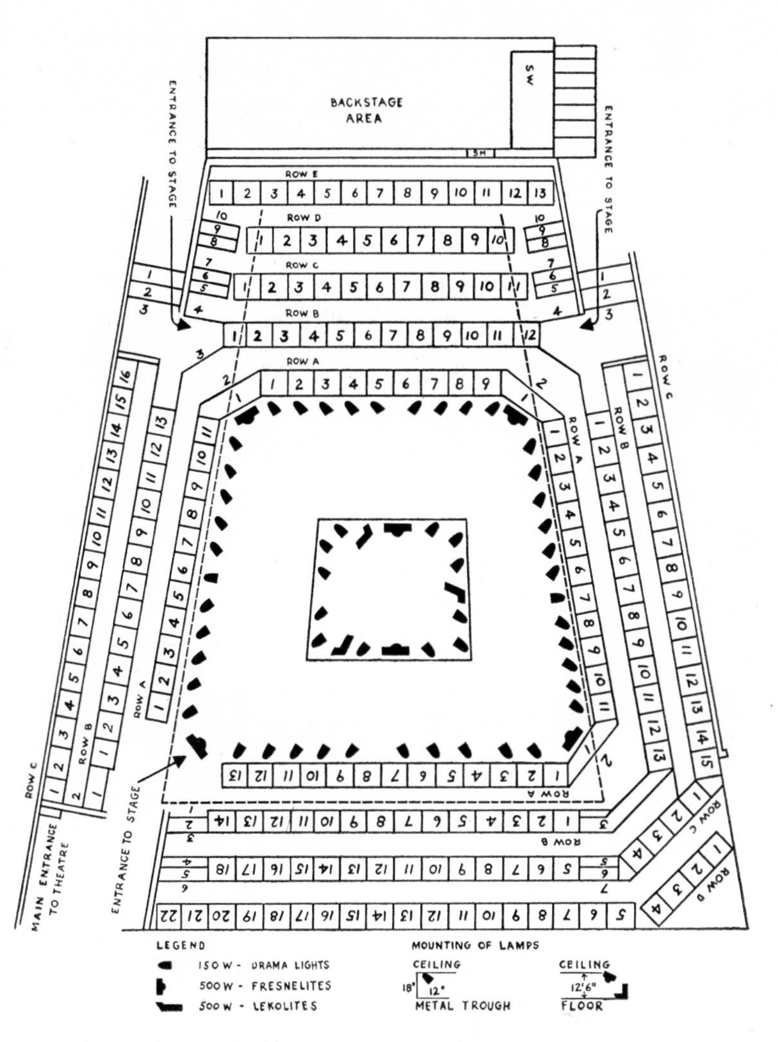

THEATRE '50: Floor and Light Plan
(Prepared by Marshall Yokelson)

THEATRE '50: Chekhov's THE SEA GULL (*Wilson Brooks, Mary Finney, Rebecca Hargis*)

THEATRE '50: Dorothy Parker and Ross Evans' THE COAST OF ILLYRIA (*Edwin Whitner, Rebecca Hargis, Wilson Brooks, Margaret McDonald, Romola Robb*)

THEATRE '50: Goldsmith's SHE STOOPS TO CONQUER
(*Romola Robb, Mary Finney, Jack Warden*)

THEATRE '50 production of Tennessee Williams' SUMMER AND SMOKE
(*Katherine Balfour, Tod Andrews*)

THEATRE '50: Vivian Connell's THRONG O'SCARLET (*Jack Warden, George Mitchell*)

ARENA (New York City): George Kelly's THE SHOW-OFF (From extreme right, counter-clockwise: *Jane Seymour, Lee Tracy, Carmen Mathews, Frances Waller, Joseph Holland, Archie Smith, Walter Cartwright, Howard Wendell, Dudley Sadler*)

EXIT
EXIT
EXIT

PENTHOUSE THEATRE OF THE UNIVERSITY OF WASHINGTON: Façade

PENTHOUSE THEATRE OF ATLANTA: Moss Hart's LIGHT UP THE SKY (Beginning at extreme left, clockwise: *Robert McBride,*

PENTHOUSE THEATRE OF ATLANTA: Rachel Crothers' LET US BE GAY (*Joel Ashley, Jean Barnes, George Englund, Kay Francis*)

ARENA (New York City) : Shakespeare's JULIUS CAESAR
(*Basil Rathbone, Joseph Holland*)

does not find when the evening is broken up into several plays. Feeling, however, that the three Tennessee Williams plays—*Portrait of a Madonna, This Property Is Condemned* and *The Last of My Solid Gold Watches*—have a unity of quality if not of story, I decided to put them on. The triple bill was well received by the press, but it did not seem to be as satisfactory to the public as our full-length presentations. Theatre '50, however, is proud to have produced them.

The Last of My Solid Gold Watches is set in a shabby hotel bedroom in a small Mississipi town in 1938, and the protagonist is Mr. Charlie Colton, a shoe salesman aged seventy-eight, "the last of the Delta drummers." The world has changed, and he no longer is able to sell his ware; neither the customer nor the product is the same any more. "My pockets are full of watches," he says, "which tell me that my time's just about over!" (He had won fifteen watches at the annual sales conventions of his company for being their outstanding drummer.) The young salesman, to whom Mr. Charlie recounts his glorious days and complains about the present ("The emphasis isn't on quality. Production, production, yes! But out of inferior goods!"), becomes bored and walks out on the old man. Mr. Charlie invites the porter to reminisce with him about the good old days, and the porter, nodding, replies: "The graveyard is crowded with folks we knew, Mistuh Charlie."

To create the physical environment of the dilapidated hotel room we centered the action around one main piece of furniture, an old-fashioned iron bedstead; although the head was high, there were no sightline problems because the audience could see everything through the bars. The room was rounded out with a worn-out rug, a cuspidor, a rocker and a low chest topped with a porcelain washbasin and pitcher.

At the end of this play, we completely cleared the stage for *This Property Is Condemned,* one of Mr. Williams's most touching short dramas. The central character of this two-character play is a thirteen-year-old girl named Willie who wears her late sister's clothes and make-up and dreams of following in her footsteps. It is apparent to the onlooker that Willie's sister was a lady of easy virtue, but the child has glamorized every tawdry and cheap experience the dead girl ever had. And as she "starts back along the railroad track, weaving grotesquely to keep her balance," and singing her sister's sad little sentimental tune ("You're the only star in my blue heaven"), we know what she will inevitably become, and we wish that somehow the world could be a better place to live in.

We used absolutely no furniture or scenery for this play. The railroad track was imagined by the actress playing Willie as well as by the audience, and our neutral-colored carpeting became the ground. The stage was set with the little girl's costume, her doll, the lighting and mood music. We also found a steel-guitar version of the song which she sings, and played it as the lights went down.

For the third play, *Portrait of a Madonna,* we had to go back to a hotel setting, this time an apartment in a shabby genteel hotel inhabited by Miss Lucretia Collins. To achieve the feeling of the neglect and disorder which surround Miss Collins, the room was portrayed very naturalistically, cluttered with chairs, books, old records, sheet music, stationery, crumpled letters and notes and just garbage.

It is in this atmosphere that Lucretia, a spinster who used to be assistant to the Sunday School superintendent, has lived for years, imagining that every night a man she once loved comes into her room and "indulges his senses." As long as her money lasted, the hotel manager was willing to put up with her; but now that she is penniless, she is being committed to an institution. She leaves with the delusion that she is expecting a child. Tennessee Williams has combined tragedy and the grotesque in such a way that the overwhelming feeling for Miss Collins at the end of the play must be one of deep compassion.

THRONG O'SCARLET, *by Vivian Connell.*

I had wanted to produce Mr. Connell's *The Nineteenth Hole of Europe,* but this was the one play I decided would be inadvisable to stage in a small theatre-in-the-round because of the horror and gore the audience would have to face at close range; I felt that this might so unnerve them that the total impact of the play, which I greatly admire, would be lost.

But I also liked another one of Mr. Connell's plays, *Throng O'Scarlet* and was happy to be able to do it. It is set in and near a country house in South Cork, Ireland, and revolves around the people connected with a fox hunt. This is a lusty drama, full of love-making as well as hounds and horses and foxes, and quite different in spirit and approach from any other play we have done.

Throng presented us with one of our toughest production problems. Its four sets represented, respectively, a high-class drawing room, an Irish pub, a saddle room and the slaughter-shed at the kennels. Both scenes of the first act take place in the drawing room, which was done with complete realism and struck during the intermission. For the first scene of the second act the stage was set for the pub: two tables, with four chairs around each, and a low bar (the bartender had to sit behind the bar because if he stood, he would obstruct the sightlines). To turn this pub into the saddle room for the second scene of the same act, we struck the bar, placed several saddles in the room for atmosphere, and covered the tables with tablecloths since the room was to be used for a picnic. This was done very rapidly, and so was the next change, which took us to the slaughterhouse. We used our "camouflage" method and covered every piece of furniture with burlap, struck the saddles, set a cot near the center of the area and hit this center with a spotlight, leaving the rest of the stage in semidarkness. The entire set was again shifted after the second act was over, and the realistic drawing room was put back in place. For the last scene of the play, however, we had to return to the pub, and again a complete but very swift change was required. By organizing each move very carefully and rehearsing the whole procedure at length, we managed to waste a minimum of time and sustain the illusion of the play for the audience.

Sound effects took care of the fox barking in the distance, but one of the characters has to blow a fox-horn on stage, and the actor had to learn to do it believably.

The slaughter-shed scene included a pot of meat which was being readied for the hounds and a dead horse which attracted rats. How well the audience responded to these elements (imaginary, of course) is recounted by George Mitchell in his article: ". . . an actor stamped his feet suddenly and shouted, 'Can't we do something about these rats!' Nobody ran out of the theatre, but I swear that every feminine front-rower drew up her feet at least fourteen inches from the stage floor."

THE TAMING OF THE SHREW, *by William Shakespeare.*

This was our first Shakespearean production, and it proved such a delight to both the audience and the actors that we resolved to do an Elizabethan play every season if possible.

I believe that Shakespeare is the greatest playwright of all times, but I do not approach his work with awe. The insight into human nature and the great poetry are a stimulus to any director or actor, but there is a danger in worshiping Shakespeare too much and treating him as pure literature. The Shakespearean plays were written for a popular audience and when presented today they should be clear and interesting to the spectator, for I do not believe there are many people who come to the theatre merely "to hear the great words." The reason Shakespeare's plays have survived and will continue to survive is that he is the most universal author who ever wrote for the theatre. He deals with the basic elements in character, and these do not change.

The Taming of the Shrew, for example, is a lively farce-comedy about the battle of the sexes with the resulting triumph of the male. It is full of humor in both line and situation, and from the indications in the verse the director and the actors can create a wealth of pantomime.

I eliminated the induction of the play because I saw no reason for a framework in an intimate theatre. There is no need for a Christopher Sly in a theatre where 198 people are on the stage with the actors; in a manner of speaking, they are all Christopher Slys and could be told:

> . . . they thought it good you hear a play
> And frame your mind to mirth and merriment,
> Which bars a thousand harms and lengthens life.

The words, however, were not essential. The audience was on the same level with the actors, and the stage was set for the story of Katharina and Petruchio.

Not much more of the script was cut. Among Shakespeare's early comedies, *Shrew* is probably the best plotted and the one in which the characterizations are best realized. I do feel it is important in planning a Shakespearean production to work from the originals and arrive at your own cuttings rather than use one of the many acting versions which may contain deviations from Shakespeare which you would not choose to take.

Our setting depended entirely on the lights and costumes. The furniture consisted of four white benches and a table for the scenes in Petruchio's house. A mock top was placed on this table for the banquet scene.

Setting the stage for the banquet was made part of the action of the play, for the servants were changing the position of the benches, bringing in stools and setting the mock table in place while they were waiting for Petruchio's entrance. The short scenes in a Shakespearean play have to acquire a fluidity so that there are no long waits and, if possible, none at all. By designing movement for the servants with musical accompaniment it is possible to give the play a flow from scene to scene comparable to the fade-out and fade-in and dissolve of a movie.

We found out for the first time that the audience can be frightened if swords are brandished too close to their faces, and also that fight scenes have to be staged with great skill and split-second timing in order to seem real and not hurt the performers.

Our approach to Grumio was rather unconventional. He was played by a big, athletic-looking actor, who wore a costume which was a ludicrous replica of Petruchio's.

In the last scene of the play, when Katharina speaks as the converted, obedient and docile wife, she circled around the banquet table, addressing the other characters over their shoulders or to their face, as the case might be, an example of "making the rounds" in this medium with perfect motivation. For Katharina gradually talks to all of them:

> Fie, fie! unknit that threatening unkind brow;
> And dart not scornful glances from those eyes,
> To wound thy lord, thy king, thy governor:
> It blots thy beauty as frosts do bite the meads,
> Confounds thy fame as whirlwinds shake fair buds,
> And in no sense is meet or amiable.
>
> I am ashamed that women are so simple
> To offer war where they could kneel for peace;
> Or seek for rule, supremacy and sway,
> When they are bound to serve, love and obey.

And as she winds up with Petruchio:

> Then vail your stomachs, for it is no boot,
> And place your hands below your husband's foot:

In token of which duty, if he please,
My hand is ready, may it do him ease.

LEMPLE'S OLD MAN, *by Manning Gurian.*

The spirit of youth is not restricted to the young in age. Why cannot an old man be a Western Union messenger? Why can he not take ballet lessons if he chooses? It is wonderful to see the old enjoying life as much or more than the young with a carefree, healthy attitude. That is what *Lemple's Old Man* said in terms of a light comedy with farcical overtones.

The set represents the sidewalk and front steps of a house in Brooklyn. We used park benches and a fire hydrant to suggest the sidewalk and placed street lamps at two of our entrances; the three steps at the end of one of the aisleways were the front steps of the house.

A block party took place in the play and called for putting up decorations and electrical equipment to prepare the street; a number of Japanese lanterns served the purpose and changed the appearance of the sidewalk for that scene.

Lemple's old man makes his first entrance on a bicycle saying, "Look, no feet!" We opened the double doors of our floor level entrance and the actor rode in and circled the playing area on his bicycle, creating the effect the author had wanted.

Since the old man was an inventor of sorts, some

gag props were necessary, and they can be used in this intimate theatre even though the audience is so close. For instance, one of his inventions was an alarm clock which made orange juice when it went off; with some skillful faking, the oranges seemed to be in a process of being squeezed in a box under the gadget.

One of the characters had to paint a picture on the stage; for this purpose we obtained an almost completed painting and had the actor fill in a few strokes during every performance.

Our main problem with this play, however, was to create an authentic Brooklyn-street-scene atmosphere with the variety of accents and dialects the author described, but our actors were flexible and versatile enough to transport their Dallas audience eastward.

THE IMPORTANCE OF BEING EARNEST, *by Oscar Wilde.*

Oscar Wilde was eager to shock a Victorian society with his epigrammatic satire, but today we are more entertained by his great wit than by his perverse criticism of his contemporaries. Because Wilde always remembered, in this play, to be amusing, the satire never becomes bitter; as Eric Bentley has said in *The Playwright as Thinker*: "Before the enemy can denounce Wilde the agile outburst is over and [we] are back among the cucumber sandwiches."

Although the story of the play follows the pattern

of nineteenth-century sentimental melodrama, the spirit in which it is written cries out for a high comedy approach, not unlike that of the Restoration theatre.

Our production was highly stylized. Color ran rampant in the costuming, and the movement was almost like the choreography for a ballet. The three settings consisted of furniture which was also very stylized and brightly upholstered.

In the second act Cecily waters her rose garden; she merely had to go through the motions since there was no attempt at realism. She cut an artificial pink rose to put in Algernon's buttonhole. And she sat on a circular bench which is supposed to surround a tree which was not there; but it was sufficient to have Cecily look at it as if it stood there, and the audience saw it, too.

Algernon consumes a tremendous amount of food in acts one and two: cucumber sandwiches first and muffins later. The use of extremely small waferlike pieces of bread enabled the actor to eat one after another and get each one down in one swallow.

In this production we played music only between acts. When Algernon played the piano in an adjoining room, a recording was utilized.

I believe *The Importance of Being Earnest* is a good play for any theatre to produce, and it is ideal for a repertory company. It never fails to entertain the audience and provides the actors and the director with an opportunity to exercise their inventiveness in stylizing the production.

LEAF AND BOUGH, *by Joseph Hayes.*

Set in a farming community in Indiana, near the Ohio River, *Leaf and Bough* speaks of the efforts of two young people to run away from the dullness and narrowness of their surroundings. It is a basically realistic play with touches of poetic imagery and a strong feeling of nostalgia. The character studies of Nan and Mark, the girl and the boy of the story, as well as those of their respective families form a heartbreaking gallery of human beings in the process of being destroyed by their own weaknesses. But the play is not pessimistic, for the two young protagonists fight their way out, and as the final scene ends, there is definite hope for their future.

The play has four simultaneous sets (the greatest number of any production we have done): a mountaintop, a street scene and the interiors of Nan's and Mark's homes. The kitchen of one house and the living room of the other necessitated only a few chairs, a table, a sofa. An aisleway became the street, and the mountaintop was represented by a small platform about three feet high, covered with neutral-colored carpeting. This involved a mixture of styles because the mountaintop was not the least bit realistic, and the interiors were; but the necessary believability was established for the audience, and that is all that matters.

In order to avoid long waits when moving from one area to another, we used mood music which would begin playing before the end of a scene. As the music started, the players appearing in the following scene made their entrance very quietly into a dimly lit area (but in full view of the audience) and took their positions. The lights went down on the first scene and up on the next scene with the mood music continuing and gradually fading out as the scene got under way.

An off-stage carnival was suggested with a record of hurdy-gurdy music and some yelling mingled with normal conversation.

The kitchen was supplied with a stove which had to be small (obviously each area could take up only very little space) and still make the audience believe that a meal could be cooked on it. Since it is highly impractical to wash dishes on this type of staging (unless very naturalistically done, it would break the illusion of reality for the spectator), we made a low homemade sink with a top, and the dishes were placed inside for later washing.

The challenge this play presented was having to knit the scenes together without throwing the audience out of the mood, and we accomplished this by making our stage completely fluid with the aid of light and music. It was such a complicated production that it led a play agent who visited us at the time to say that, if theatre-in-the-round could put on *Leaf and Bough,* it had no limitations whatsoever. And, indeed, our plans for the future include such productions as *Peer Gynt* and *A Midsummer Night's Dream.*

BLACK JOHN, *by Barton MacLane.*

The time is 1905; the place, Lyme Cushing's saloon on Halfaday Creek in the Yukon. The play is a rough and raucous farce which is also a take-off on an old-fashioned melodrama.

Halfaday Creek is a refuge of men wanted by the law. Since so many of them have adopted the name John Smith, they can only identify each other by qualifying their first names; we have, therefore, a "Black John," a "Red John," a "One-Eye John" and a "One-Arm John." We have also a dashing hero who is a corporal in the Canadian Mounted Police, a heroine who is a dance-hall girl, bandits and a henpecked farmer pursued by his shrewish wife; these people, among others, provide story elements, with Black John as a pivotal character who rules this community of outcasts and nearly hangs a man in the saloon before the hilarious proceedings are over.

The scaffold or "hanging beam" was erected at the end of an aisleway, and a mechanism was rigged up around the victim's body so that the weight would not be on his neck, as it appeared to be.

Perhaps the scene which the audience enjoyed the most was one in which several characters play their favorite game: betting whether or not a fly will light on a lump of sugar. The actors followed the imaginary fly with their eyes, and so did the audience, giving an added excitement to this somewhat unusual parlor entertainment.

Third Season

THE LEARNED LADIES, *by Molière*
(Charles Hidden Page translation).

I wanted to open the third season with a stylized production and chose Molière's witty high comedy, *Les Femmes Savantes,* which is done much too seldom in this country.

In this play, which is next to the last one Molière wrote before his death, the great comic returned to his earlier satirical attack on the "blue-stocking" or "précieuse" trend. Although there is a sentimental note in the resolution of the plot, I feel it is a fuller play than *Les Précieuses Ridicules* and a brilliant comedy of character. Few writers of comedy have succeeded as well as Molière in provoking a genuinely thoughtful laughter, always derived from the author's way of looking at life: intellectual rather than emotional.

The period of the play is approximately when it was written (1672), or perhaps a few years earlier, but we felt that we could achieve a higher degree of stylization, especially in our costumes, if we moved the time to

1780. It was around this period that a pastoral craze came over the wealthy classes of France and induced them to dress as shepherds and shepherdesses. Our costume designer delved into history and discovered that while brocades and damasks were typical of the late eighteenth century, wealthy French families preferred fine cotton fabrics which were imported and therefore more attractive to them. The costumes for our production were made of glazed chintz, organdie and net.

The color scheme revolved around pinks, blues and other soft pastel shades in the costumes, while the furniture (French provincial especially painted to maintain the pastoral tone) was upholstered in white quilted chintz.

Philaminte, the middle-aged pedant who decides to undertake the study of philosophy, and her "*précieuses*" daughter and sister-in-law wore blue with the blue stockings symbolizing women's equality to men (which Molière, of course, seeks to disprove in this play).

When an actress wears a hat with a wide brim—as a few did in this production—it is advisable to take the hat off soon after arriving on the stage because the brim covers the actress's face for a large portion of the audience. The same applies to a very tall hat.

To unify the set we hung a papier-mâché balloon in the center of the acting area and from it a basket full of flowers (which were fresh roses on opening night); this was an added colorful touch which rounded out the physical production and helped to recreate the period of the play.

The movement was handled very much like dance, for these people in their very frivolous pastoral costumes were like graceful marionettes in a ballroom environment.

HERE'S TO US! *by Shirland Quin.*

We followed the Molière play with a modern comedy which takes place during twenty-four hours in June in the Gramercy Park apartment of a literary agent named Kit Tremaine.

Miss Quin's brittle drawing-room comedy deals with the world of Kit Tremaine, which includes the radio crowd as well as literary agents and their cohorts. With clever dialogue the author tells the story of how Kit sublets her New York apartment to a former test pilot who at the moment is a victim of the housing shortage; he is to occupy the place daily from dinnertime until ten in the morning, at which time Kit returns from commuting to New Rochelle and begins her everyday routine (the apartment serves as her office, too). The rest of the play is concerned with how the two almost, but not quite, became lovers.

The play presented only one minor technical problem. A character was supposed to be feeding pigeons at a window. A French window was simply imagined at the end of an aisleway and the actor threw morsels to the pigeons as they were on a terrace off stage. A record took care of the pigeon's response.

Since one of the characters in the play is a radio commentator, and his voice is heard over the air at one point, we made a special recording for this purpose.

TWELFTH NIGHT, *by William Shakespeare.*

Our second Shakespearean production offers an excellent example of how the Bard set the stage with words.

"Enter Viola, a Captain, and Sailors.
VIOLA: What country, friends, is this?
CAPTAIN: This is Illyria, lady."

And Illyria it is, though the playing area contains nothing but three benches.

Twelfth Night is a romantic comedy which includes broad humor and satire as well as romance, and a production must find a way of combining all the various elements into a harmonious whole. It should be the story of the disguised Viola, of the ridiculed Malvolio, of the boisterous Sir Toby Belch, of the clown. Allardyce Nicoll, in *World Drama,* writes about Shakespeare's comedy of romance: "There is a kind of transcendentalism here, where the objective and the subjective meet; where the author is at one with his characters and yet, godlike, above them; where intellectual laughter becomes emotional; where clowns become wise and wise men fools. We scoff at ridiculous absurdities in these plays and discover that we are mocking ourselves . . ."

As in *The Taming of the Shrew,* we used a minimum of furniture and emphasized the color and wit of the costumes. In searching for a style in costuming, we arrived at a design resembling a spirit of Mardi Gras, which went beautifully with the comic action of the play.

The permanent setting consisted of three black benches, to which a table and a stool were added for the drinking scenes; these pieces were brought in by Sir Toby and Sir Andrew themselves and were struck at the end of the act.

For Malvolio's prison scene, we used the second window in the control booth. This meant, of course, that the spectators sitting in the five rows below the control booth could not see Malvolio without craning, but they could hear him and the visual emphasis was thrown on Feste, who was addressing the jailed Malvolio. Feste moved from the playing area itself up the steps and into the audience.

When Malvolio finds the love letter in the garden ("To the unknown beloved, this, and my good wishes—") and reads it aloud to himself, his three observers (Toby, Andrew and Fabian) moved to the end of the aisleway and stooped behind the railing, raising their heads every now and then. During the reading, they would occasionally steal into the center, almost peer over Malvolio's shoulder and return to their place of hiding.

The fluidity of the production was achieved in the same way as in *Shrew,* and again a great deal of music was played. We opened the play with Feste singing as he does at the conclusion. A small spot lighted him as he started singing; then the light spread and Feste continued his song, moving around and addressing it directly to the audience, accompanying himself on a fake mandolin.

The arrival of the New Year, 1949, was celebrated with this production. The performance ended shortly before midnight, and the ensuing festivities with serpentine and confetti were very much in the spirit of the play.

SKAAL, *by Vivian Johannes.*

Skaal is a drama set against the background of the big-woods country north of the Mississippi Valley, and the time is the end of the nineteenth century. Into this Norwegian settlement a young man brings his bride, and several clashes arise as a result. Though the play has some incidents of great dramatic power, it depends largely on mood and atmosphere.

The play has three sets: a kitchen, a clearing beyond the kitchen door and a millhouse. The kitchen had to be quite realistic with numerous pots and pans and a good stove, for there is a considerable amount of cooking and baking in the script. The clearing was suggested by camouflaging the kitchen set with burlap, a procedure similar to that employed in *Throng O'Scarlet.* The millhouse was also created with camouflage plus the introduction of a few characteristic pieces like an anvil and a knife sharpener.

The storm, the wind, the forest fire were all effected with recordings. The music, on the other hand, was partially recorded and partially played on stage. For instance, there is a scene in which one of the characters plays the "Blue Danube" on the accordion, which the actor learned to play. The accordion music makes the protagonist dance, and as she does, she reminisces. Now, the "Blue Danube" comes over the amplifier, and the boy stops playing his accordion on stage; when the girl's memory returns to the present, the actor resumes his playing, This required a great deal of rehearsing, but the emotional effect made it well worth it.

STING IN THE TAIL, *by Tom Purefoy.*

The title of the play refers to the effects of wasp poison, which is what gets this Irish farce started. Norah Despard has calmly murdered her husband; her brother wants to maintain the family reputation at all costs, and therefore seeks a way to prove that Norah's husband died a natural death. A clever spinster takes over, and the macabre rapidly becomes humorous. As John Rosenfield put it in his review, it is " . . . a tongue-in-cheek murder plot laced with old arsenic."

Since the setting is a sitting room "somewhere in the British Isles" and most probably in Ireland and the time is 1905, Victorian furniture and costumes were appropriate. The play presented no special problems.

THE SEA GULL, *by Anton Chekhov.*
(Stark Young translation).

The Stark Young texts make Chekhov comprehensible and not at all remote for an American audience, and they preserve the original of Chekhov. In his preface, Mr. Young calls the play ". . . a translation; it is not an adaptation. No speech has been moved out of the place where Chekhov put it and, with the exception here and there of little odds and ends that might come to three of four lines, nothing has been cut." The translator also points out that Chekhov is not the least bit obscure in the original and: "As for any simplification, my sorest struggle was to get my lines as simple as Chekhov's—a difficult problem because such simplicity must rest on great precision. Of the two, Chekhov's dialogue is perhaps a trifle more colloquial than mine. Certainly in places it is more colloquial than I should ever dare to be; for in a translation any very marked colloquialism is always apt to hurt the economy of effect by raising questions as to what the original could have been to come out so patly as that."

In Mr. Young's text Chekhov's wonderful gift for combining tragedy and comedy comes clearly to the fore, and at last Madame Arcadina, her unfortunate son, Nina, Trigorin and the others become real people. This is a factor of vital importance for any production of *The Sea Gull;* the pathos of the characters' lives must never become so gloomy that the audience will find it laughable. The correct proportions are in the Stark Young translation, and it is up to the director to follow its indications.

A play with a great deal of detail, in which every character's movement and the rhythm of every word count, it is ideally suited for an intimate theatre. We were faced with only one technical difficulty, the location of the stage on which Nina performs in the first act. We put up a small curtain in front of our floor-level entrance (the one with the double doors), and behind it there was an eight-foot platform. As the curtain was about to open, the lights went down on the central acting area, and a spot illuminated the play within the play.

In this play we also used a candelabrum with real candles.

We found it was possible to reduce the number of settings from four to two: the garden and a sitting room in Sorin's house. Both were done quite realistically, although the garden scene depended largely on lighting to give it the required atmosphere.

SHE STOOPS TO CONQUER, *by Oliver Goldsmith.*

To counteract the implausibility of the basic situation of this farce, I felt that it should be treated as a big romp, played very rapidly and very broadly.

While the scenery remained simple (benches, stools and tables, like those we used in the Shakespearean productions), the costumes were hooked up in color, line and ornament, especially Tony Lumpkin's.

The few pieces of furniture were moved as part of the action, and no attempt at all was made to create any realism in the settings of the Hardcastle home, the ale house or the garden.

Many members of our audience remarked after seeing the play that it was amazing how well this Eighteenth Century farce looked in the round, considering that it was written for a picture-frame theatre when this type of stage was a novelty!

THE COAST OF ILLYRIA, *by Dorothy Parker and Ross Evans.*

We were very happy to be able to give this play its première performance, for in addition to its dramatic power, it is a script of outstanding literary value.

Set in an intellectual milieu of nineteenth-century London and centering around the broken lives of Charles and Mary Lamb, the play takes its title from the Lambs' version of *Twelfth Night*: "There were a brother and sister who were shipwrecked off the coast of Illyria." For Charles and Mary Lamb, the coast of Illyria is the edge of sanity or normalcy, for they have to live on the fringe of the world.

To save Mary from a mental institution (Bedlam,

to be exact) after she has killed their mother, Charles agrees to take care of her for the rest of his life. The play considers the tragedy of Mary, a brilliant woman and a very warm person, who knows that she has periods of derangement. And it speaks of Charles's sacrifice, clearly illustrated when he has to break off his romance with the actress Fanny Kelly in order to devote his time to his diseased sister.

The authors of *The Coast of Illyria* have also drawn the whole literary atmosphere of the Romantic period and have peopled their drama with the words and personalities of Coleridge, Hazlitt and DeQuincey as well as the Lambs. Their wit, their intelligence and their anguishes are reflected in the action of the play.

We discovered that a "mad scene" can be very effective in theatre-in-the-round, for Mary Lamb has one of her periodic attacks in the course of the play and is held down by the other characters. The intimacy of the medium made the scene more intense and more moving.

The Lambs' flat, furnished in the Empire period, was probably the most naturalistic setting we have ever had in our theatre. Our intention was to make the audience feel at once that this was a room in which Charles and Mary lived, studied, read, wrote and had gatherings with the outstanding intellects of their time. Low bookcases lined the imaginary walls, and every book, pen stand and figurine was authentic. Since many of these were costly antiques and had to be borrowed, we carried heavy insurance on them (as we do on all borrowed properties).

Fourth Season

HEARTBREAK HOUSE, *by George Bernard Shaw.*

The play, which Shaw endows with the subtitle "A Fantasia in the Russian Manner on English Themes," was first produced in 1919, but the playwright says in his preface:

"*Heartbreak House* is not merely the name of the play which follows this preface. It is cultured, leisured Europe before the war. When the play was begun, not a shot had been fired; and only the professional diplomatists and the very few amateurs whose hobby is foreign policy even knew that the guns were loaded. A Russian playwright, Tchekov, had produced four fascinating dramatic studies of *Heartbreak House*, of which three, *The Cherry Orchard, Uncle Vanya*, and *The Seagull*, had been performed in England."

Allardyce Nicoll compares this Shavian work with the plays of Chekhov in his *World Drama*: "It is as though, in place of the individualized persons whom the Russian dramatist had loved to gather together in one limited locale, Shaw had taken his method and peopled his house with ideas—the idea of the out-of-date conservative, the idea of the new financier, the idea of the purposeless woman of the world. The atmospheres of *The Cherry Orchard* and of *Heartbreak House* have much in common—a mingled nostalgia for something rather lovely that is perishing and a dim hope for the future, a combination of contempt for moral helplessness and of admiration for courage; but whereas we come from Chekhov's plays with certain human characters indelibly implanted in our minds, from Shaw's we come with vivid memories of basic philosophies trenchantly expressed."

I felt an impulse to do this play because it is incredibly timely for a drama written before World War I, and it is as prophetic today (if not more so) as when it was first conceived.

We played *Heartbreak House* in contemporary costumes and did not cut or alter a single line, although the play is somewhat too long. Captain Shotover, whose age is eighty, was believably but subtly made up. The catastrophic air raid of the last act was handled with lights and sound effects.

AN OLD BEAT-UP WOMAN, *by Sari Scott.*

During our third season, Sari Scott submitted a one-act play to me which I found thoroughly exciting, and I asked the author to consider the possibility of turning it into a full-length script. About midsummer Miss Scott came up with a new version of the play, which was a closer investigation of her characters rather than a mere expansion. I had felt in reading the original draft that there was a great deal more to be said about Miss Scott's people. The author was with us for six weeks prior to the opening of her play, and I wish it were always possible to have the playwright around for that length of time; then there is really opportunity to discuss the story, the ideas, the characters and the small details of interpretation and technique.

An Old Beat-Up Woman has only three characters: Joe Neal, a truck driver in the Texas Panhandle region (in whom the critics found a resemblance to Molnar's Liliom); Utah, his tough, warm, long-suffering but practical wife; and Pete, their friend, with whom Utah could have presumably had a happy life. Joe and Utah part and get together again, and when Utah decides to leave him for good, Joe shoots himself. Much as she loves him, Utah is glad he has committed suicide, for now he is still handsome and strong, but if he had continued his life of vagrancy and drunkenness, he would have ended up alone and dirty and ugly.

There is a theatrical poetry in the rough and tough language of these people, in their actions, in their warmheartedness and much dramatic power in the situations they create for themselves.

The set represented an "eight by twenty on skids," a house that could be moved on a truck. Although a stove and a sink were called for in the script, in this case we found it would facilitate matters to have these pieces off stage.

For Joe's suicide scene, we used an off-stage sound, but the audience was not aware of this because Joe shoots himself in a dark room and, therefore, could not be seen at the time.

A hysterical memory sequence in the second act required a tremendous change in lighting to clarify the transition to the spectators. This was accomplished by music and a recording of a sandstorm.

An Old Beat-Up Woman was produced in New Haven and Boston later in the same season, but did not reach Broadway.

ROMEO AND JULIET, *by William Shakespeare.*

For our first Shakespearean tragedy we selected the greatest love story of all time and perhaps the Bard's outstanding lyric drama. *Romeo and Juliet* shows Shakespeare to be also a master of plotting, as George Pierce Baker explains in *The Development of Shakespeare as a Dramatist*: the exposition is quick and simple in the opening quarrel scene; the movement thereafter is swift from exciting incident to exciting incident; comedy relief is provided by characters essential to the story (the Nurse, Mercutio); great care is taken in the motivation of every action; and the poetic phrase is always in character.

We found that a serious Elizabethan play appealed

as much to our audiences and played as well in the round as the comedies.

The production followed the standards of simplicity we had set with *Shrew* and *Twelfth Night.* The balcony scene was treated in the following manner: Juliet appeared at the end of an aisleway at the top of the three steps and was lighted with a pin-spot. Another pin-spot hit Romeo at the opposite end of the playing area. Shakespeare's words, as usual, set the stage, and the audience knew that Juliet was on her balcony and Romeo in the garden. Then, as the young people became aware of each other's presence (and he was supposed to go towards the balcony), both the actor and the actress moved into the center of the playing area, into a pool of light. This had now become the balcony, and the audience again accepted the stylization, supplying the architecture with their imaginations.

The play was cut so that the two scenes in Juliet's bedroom follow each other. To set the stage for them, the Capulet servants moved the four benches together and covered them with velvet; this became Juliet's bed. There was an intermission after the second bedroom scene, and the bed was struck.

For the final scene it would have been too difficult and would have taken too long to set up the tomb during a black-out. Instead, as the lights went up for that scene, the servants brought Juliet in on a couch, which, when placed in the acting area, became the tomb.

MY GRANNY VAN, *by Loren Disney and George Sessions Perry.*

The play is a dramatization of George Sessions Perry's autobiographical book, published in 1949, and has an intense regional flavor. While two of our other productions (*An Old Beat-Up Woman* and *Southern Exposure*) also had a Southern locale, *My Granny Van* is the only genuinely regional Texas play we have presented at Theatre '50.

The comedy is set in Rockdale, a small town eighteen miles east of Taylor, Texas, in 1922, and it deals with George Sessions Perry's grandmother; the author himself, at the age of eight, is a character in the play. A program note explained only four of the characters "are outright characters of the author's fancy. In the case of Miss Stephanie, residents of Rockdale might detect a resemblance to a beloved lady of that town. As regards the 'real-life characters,' the authors have no way of being one-hundred-percent sure they would have reacted as they do in the situations portrayed, but the authors feel confident, or at least hope, that such would have been the case."

The plot centers around the feud between Granny Van, an active and mischievous old lady, and her virtually senile father-in-law from Indiana. Granny is a lovable character whom the audience finds easily indentifiable; yet she has her peculiarities, such as enjoying her "med" (whiskey) while voting the prohibition ticket!

The description of the setting required a closet underneath the stairway. It could not be eliminated since it serves an important function in the play: it is the young boy's hiding place. As a substitute, we placed a large table behind a couch and covered it to the floor with an old-fashioned tablecloth; this became the boy's "pirate's den."

The old-fashioned Victrola on the set had a horn so tall that it would interfere with the sightlines even if the instrument were placed on a low table; the solution was to leave the horn on the floor until it was time to play the Victrola.

The records played on this Victrola had to be authentic ("My Pretty Red Wing" and "The Old Rugged Cross") recordings of the period.

At one point in the play Granny decides to black out her father-in-law's picture in a family group photograph. Since a good portrait had to be employed, we did not want to ruin one at every performance and so covered it with a piece of isinglass, from which Granny's pencil marks could be wiped off.

A window was erected in one corner of the theatre, since the window curtains had to be taken off by one of the characters and became an essential prop. An old-fashioned wall telephone with a crank was attached to a corner wall.

In a lively and humorous card-game scene the audience played along with the actors, and it was of great importance to stack the cards correctly before every performance.

COCK-A-DOODLE DANDY, *by Sean O'Casey.*

It was a wonderful experience to give the first professional production to this imaginative poetic fantasy by one of the greatest playwrights of our time, Sean O'Casey.

The theme of this parable is, in the words of George Jean Nathan (writing in the *New York Journal American*): ". . . the rightful joy of life and the proper dismissal from all consideration of those who would fetter it. Employing a gay mixture of symbolism and wild humor, some of it as rich in laughs as anything I've read in a long time, O'Casey filters through his natural cynicism as lively and amusing a slice of fantastic drama as one can imagine. The embodiment of his central idea in the figure of a rooster, his two boozy counterparts of the memorable Fluther and Joxer, his fancy in such scenes as those in which the fairest and most delicate of his females suddenly sprouts devil's horns, and in which the stern males madly try to bag an innocent little fowl which they superstitiously imagine is a creature of prodigious evil—these, and more, all coated with the brilliant writing for which the author is famous, combine to provide the kind of evening we too seldom are privileged to enjoy in the theatre of today."

The set represents a garden and a portion of Michael Marthraun's house. Some stylized patches of grass and flowers suggested the garden, and the house was symbolized by the second window in the control booth. When the whole house is supposed to shake, we shook the entire control booth.

There is a wealth of magic trickery in the play. When a man turned into a top hat, we had a black-out; a collapsible chair was used, and at times (when it was not supposed to collapse) it was replaced by a normal chair; when a bottle of liquor became obstinate and refused to pour, an alternate bottle with a stopper was hidden under the table amidst the greenery and was easily exchangeable with the first one; to make the liquor change color, the bottle was placed over a hole in the table which was equipped underneath with a red light; when a strong wind blew people over, the actors heard the sound effect and bent over as if there actually were a wind.

Yes, magic can be created in theatre-in-the-round as long as there are active imaginations at work. And now we know that we can do fantasy too.

GHOSTS, *by Henrik Ibsen.*

Our third Ibsen production also fitted the intimate style, but it was not as well liked by the public. The theme of the play is still valid today (conventions can and frequently do imprison the individual, impeding his progress and denying him both integrity and happiness), but the dramatic illustrations seem somewhat dated today. Because of the universal impact of what the play states, I still believe it is worth reviving.

THE GOLDEN PORCUPINE, *by Muriel Roy Bolton.*

This historical drama was written before the author's novel of the same name, and an earlier version of the script was produced at the Playbox in Pasadena under the title *Breath of Kings.*

Set in the fifteenth-century France of Louis XI, *The Golden Porcupine* has for its central conflict the duel of politics and sex between Anne of France, protecting her weakling brother (Charles VIII), and the man she loved (Louis of Orleans).

The three original sets were reduced to two: the King's study and a prison cell. The furniture in the royal study was covered with velvet and a royal crest was embroidered on the fabric. In order to shift to the prison cell, a few pieces were struck and the others were covered with burlap instead of velvet; of course, the lighting was changed too.

Since the portrait of a king was constantly referred to, we found it necessary to hang it in one of the corners.

The costuming was largely responsible for creating the physical atmosphere of the play. We preserved period authenticity and used a great deal of variety; Anne of France, for example, had five costume changes during the play.

The passing of twenty-eight years in the course of the evening requires changes in make-up. Subtle changes in facial make-up were effected, but the emphasis was placed on modifying the women's hair-dos; when the change had to be made between scenes, mock pieces were added or eliminated.

SOUTHERN EXPOSURE, *by Owen Crump.*

Mr. Crump's comedy is a satire on the old South, as it is preserved in Natchez, and on the tourists who visit it annually. The author's foreword reads as follows:

"High on the picturesque bluffs over the Mississippi River stands Natchez, once the pride of a great cotton empire, the center of romance and adventure during the steamboat days, and the Queen city of social and cultural life in the Old Southwest.

"Modern Natchez, which is the background of our play, numbers among its greatest assets, many fine mansions of Colonial and antebellum periods. To anyone visiting the city, the famous old houses exert a fascinating attraction, and in the spirit of preserving traditions of hospitality, and with justifiable civic pride, the Chamber of Commerce, in co-operation with leading hotels, has arranged tours that any visitor may take for a small charge.

"The climax of the season in Natchez is the advent of the Pilgrimage.

'We've got three industries in Natchez—
Cotton, Oil, and the Pilgrimage . . .'

"During the month of March, thousands upon thousands of visitors come to the city for the express purpose of taking the tours through the old homes, and to celebrate with the descendants of the old families, as they don their antebellum costumes and live again in the gracious reminiscences of the past."

The upstairs living room of one of the mansions, where the penniless Miss Penelope Mayweather holds on to her old traditons, is the setting of the play. Her struggle to keep her home and the romance she quite unknowingly engenders between a young cousin of hers and a Yankee writer are the foundations upon which the hilarious story of the play rests.

Three times during the play groups of tourists arrive to inspect the Mayweather mansion, and we found that crowds could be well managed even in a small theatre-in-the-round provided they were not left standing in one place. They moved around the playing area, sometimes almost completely surrounding Miss Penelope, but the focus remained on her throughout.

Southern Exposure, with which we closed our fourth season, was the most resounding success we have had at Theatre '50.

The Future: A Dream and a Plan

Great civilizations of the past have been judged by their culture; if ours is to go on record as a great civilization, we must match our mechanical progress with our cultural development. And a part of this cultural development is the propagation of theatre throughout the world. It is more than a dream; it is a necessity, and it must be accomplished.

I would like to think that if I decided to take a cross-country trip along in 1960 I could stop in every city with a population of seventy-five thousand and see a good play well done. I would like to see *Othello* in Philadelphia, and a new play by a promising young American author in Pittsburgh, and *Tartuffe* in Detroit, and a new play by an established American playwright in Dayton, and *The Wild Duck* in Kansas City, and a new play by an interesting European author in Oakland, California. I would like to find in all these towns (and in all the others too) artists with ideals, and contemporary theatres, delighting their audiences every night with the best plays of the past and present. I would like all that, and I believe it can happen.

Our preoccupation should be with creating good theatre. The potential audiences are everywhere. And this is where serious theatre people have to come in and bring to these audiences the great theatre that can be theirs. A seed needs to be planted today with all the talent, materials, ideas and dreams we possess.

I am not interested in dreams without action. I will be impatient no longer. I have a definite plan for the future.

Philosophically and artistically, I believe in a better world, one in which there is mutual understanding among peoples and in which the individual has the opportunity to do what he chooses, both personally and professionally. A great amount of theatre of high quality will aid its participants—which includes the audience—in the realization of their potential power to do good and be happy.

Through the presentation of many plays, from all countries, from the past and the present, people gain knowledge, and knowledge is the greatest liberator in the world. I want our age to be a golden age in which knowledge and beauty are available to everyone. I want this age to be a golden age because selfishly I want to be a part of a civilization which is constantly being enriched. I like living in the age of the airplane and television, and I want to live in an age when there is great theatre everywhere.

Theatre '50 is now established. It must improve. My first aim is to create in Dallas a fine, imaginative theatre, full of wonderment and beauty. Unless this is done, my other plans would not have much meaning. With this in mind, I shall do my utmost to raise the standards of Theatre '50. Staying at the same level is not enough of a goal for an idealistic, progressive theatre. I will spare no effort to locate fine plays, and I will try to produce the very best of them. I will hire a staff and an acting company of the highest possible caliber, and I am in the planning process of providing Theatre '50 with greater physical facilities.

I intend to build a flexible theatre in Dallas. I have learned that if you have a million-dollar idea, you can raise a million dollars. My experience in raising money has shown me that the world is glad to help you if you have a sound idea and can prove that it is sound.

Ideally a theatre building should be able to adapt itself to the special qualities of each play. A flexible theatre is the answer. I am planning to build a flexible theatre, which will make it possible to do some plays in the round, others with a proscenium, still others with a proscenium and long apron, or in any other form the script may need. Installed in the building there will be television booths, so that in time we could add the necessary facilities and plan television productions in our theatre. Arena staging is a natural for television, as Albert McCleery has already proved with his Cameo Theatre; flexible staging would provide the medium with more variety. And I believe the different media should be of assistance to one another. I would even like to consider the possibility of making a movie in our flexible theatre, perhaps using the city itself for exteriors.

A permanent professional theatre—doing new plays and classics, and making operating costs with a small surplus—is now a reality in Dallas and the possibility of a reality everywhere else. Hundreds of arena theatres are springing up throughout the country. Very few so far are completely professional—meaning that they cannot devote as much time to the theatre as they would like—and practically none has placed emphasis on the production of new scripts. In some cases the potentiality of making money has overshadowed the determination to raise standards. The spread of the medium is not enough per se, for the medium—theatre-in-the-round—is not the answer. The answer is great theatre.

Theatre-in-the-round presents a way to start at once. It is certainly simpler and more possible to find a room which will be adaptable to this medium than to build a regular theatre at the present time. After several seasons of successfully operating a theatre-in-the-round, a city can and should work towards the building of a flexible theatre.

The very fact that theatre-in-the-round is an economical medium should make us doubly careful not to exploit it. We must use it as a way to bring about a great theatrical renaissance in America and in the world; let us remember, then, that we will never rejuvenate the theatre by doing the old things in the same old ways. In a recent letter I received from Dudley Nichols, he said: "I believe in the round theatre intensely. I believe that it is going to bring a new vitality into the American theatre . . . it can free the stage and release talents all along the line. There is so much talent that never gets a chance. . . . Dramatic talent, both acting and writing, and theatric talents too, are so much more universal than we are led to believe." Theatre-in-the-round must live up to the faith that many artists and members of the audience have in it. It may be a medium which costs less money, but it must be artistically distinguished. The re-doing of mediocre successes of the commercial theatre, the star system and the one-week rehearsal schedule will not give us the kind of theatre our audiences are waiting for and we in the theatre need. I would rather see twenty good theatres in America by 1960 than a thousand mediocre groups attempting to survive by doing things in a second-best manner. The answer, as I have said, is great theatre.

Great theatre means great writing and fine productions. We must maintain high standards and constantly give our imaginations an opportunity to improve. We must form great theatres in which there will be four absolutely inflexible basic policies:

1. Complete professionalization.

2. Production of only new plays and classics, with an emphasis on the new play.

3. A permanent resident company for the entire season.

4. A minimum of three weeks of rehearsal time for every play.

For very understandable reasons these idealistic policies (which, when they become practical, are also smart) are not being used in many places. But since it has been proved that they have succeeded in at least one place, it is evident that we must find a way to make them succeed elsewhere. There is a need for many fine professional theatres having at their helms people who believe in these policies so much that they will adhere to them regardless of any circumstances. Theoretically all good theatre people believe in them. Only the fear (a dreadful disease) of the impracticability of these policies has kept them from being used universally. This fear is dangerous; yet it is understandable because there have been instances in which experienced theatre leaders have not been able to make these policies work. These same leaders, however, are ready and willing and anxious to participate in the plans for theatres with such idealistic policies if they can be shown that said policies can and will be practical in the future.

Since I know from my own experience that they can

be practical, they are the basis of the plan I am about to describe and on which I shall be working at the time this book goes to press.

The objective of the plan is to create twenty resident professional theatres modeled after Theatre '50. This is not to be a circuit or a chain of theatres; on the contrary, each theatre should belong to its city and grow out of its community, with the added benefit of the work and experience of highly trained professional theatre people.

We all know that good legislation is beneficial, and we are anxious to pass laws which will help us progress. That is why I believe that this plan must have a basic law consisting of the four above-mentioned policies: complete professionalization; production of new plays and classics; a permanent resident company for the entire season; a minimum of three weeks of rehearsal time for each production.

To see that this basic law is observed, the project must have a policy maker, whose offices, to be located in New York City, will be the organizational and executive center of the project. The theatres in the different cities, however, will be run by individual leaders or managing directors, who will have complete authority in the selection of plays and personnel and all other matters pertaining to their theatres. These men and women can and must use their imagination and initiative; they must also believe in the basic law of this plan, and they must want its four policies to be their fundamental principles in the theatre.

The first step in my planning will be the selection of twenty cities with a population of over one hundred thousand, scattered throughout the United States of America. There are, of course, many cities which already have various forms of excellent theatre, and it follows that these will not be the cities chosen.

From a financial point of view, it will be necessary to obtain funds to pay for the services of an excellent full-time secretary, who is to work with me during the preliminary planning period. Later, it will be essential for the policy maker to have an office and office help in New York as well as traveling expenses to go to the various cities.

While the locations of the twenty theatres are being determined, I will also talk to and correspond with the people who can become the managing directors of these theatres. They will be chosen from among the experienced directors, managers, producers or other theatre workers who share with me the basic ideals of this plan. They must have the ability and background to select the manuscripts, staffs and acting companies necessary to run a first-class professional theatre. They must have taste and discretion and a great love for the theatre and progress within it. There are many professional theatre leaders in America capable of doing this job. I will find those who are in a position to do it and want to do it more than anything else.

After the planning period, it will be necessary for me to go into these twenty cities and create in each one of them a nucleus for a board of directors consisting of civic leaders, like the board that was formed to establish Theatre '50.

Once the board is set up, a place must be found in which a theatre-in-the-round can function. Such a place can be found in every city, and it must be available before a fund-raising campaign can be initiated.

The plan for the financial campaign will then be started within the board of directors, and a properly organized small financial committee will begin its activities. With proper instructions—which I will draw up, using the experience in Dallas as a basis—the sum needed (a maximum of $40,000) can be raised quickly.

As soon as the financial campaign is completed, the theatre must be leased and readied for production. At this time it will be necessary for the managing director to appear on the scene. Funds will then be available to pay his salary.

Instructions for equipping the chosen location as a theatre-in-the-round will have been prepared during the preliminary planning, and they will be presented in such a form that any skillful architect will be able to follow them and lose no time in conditioning and adjusting the theatre for arena staging.

It is undoubtedly true that for the quick success of

a theatre in one of our larger cities, it is necessary for the citizenry to accept the theatre leader at once and have a great deal of confidence in his professional ability. I believe I have found a way which will assure both the city and the managing director of the confidence of the theatre profession as a whole and which will give the managing director untold aid from a professional prestige source.

I believe that anyone who has worked in the theatre or attended the theatre in the course of the last twenty years will agree with me that the good plays we have seen in New York, the good plays toured throughout the country, the good plays transferred to the motion pictures, the good plays released for stock and amateur rights have been largely the result of the work of a vast number of New York producers. These are the people whose taste and courage have brought into our theatre most of the new playwrights and directors and designers and the finest acting in America. These men and women have had a responsibility, and through good times and bad times they have fulfilled it to the best of their ability. It has been necessary for them to be centered in the largest city of our nation, and their activities demand that they remain there, for it is important that these people continue what they are doing. They have many new plans every day, and they assume enormous responsibilities in their city and in their nation.

But I know many of them and I know some of them well, and all of them believe in good professional theatre all over the United States. They also believe in a policy of new plays and classics with an emphasis on the new play, since this is the policy they have been following on Broadway for many years.

While these men and women cannot be expected to go into the various cities and start new theatres, they can help with their experience and theatre wisdom and their knowledge of running a first-class professional theatre. And every one of them will be anxious to do anything he or she can to aid the American theatre. They have proved this.

It is important to understand clearly that these people are not to contribute to this project financially. Although many of them have made money in the theatre, they have often put it back into the theatre, and they are constantly planning productions for New York and the road which demand all their resources and the resources of the backers who have faith in them.

To expect much time and any money from this source would be impractical and in the final analysis harmful to the well-being of the professional theatre. But there is something they can do with very little time, no money and without having to leave New York City.

When the twenty theatres are virtually ready for production, with twenty directors in New York ready to start casting and to choose the new scripts and classics they want to do, the producers can be of great help to this project, to the American theatre and perhaps, in the long run, also to themselves.

Let us say that one of these talented and experienced producers is willing to act as the advisory director—entailing responsibility only to the extent he wants to assume it—of a theatre in city X. His name alone as advisory director would automatically give prestige to the venture. The producer, through his years of work in the theatre, has great knowledge about the selection of plays and the availability of good personnel. In a very short time he could advise and aid the managing director in the hiring of a business manager (a member of the union, of course) and a director (that is, in case the managing director himself is not to direct). Through his casting department the producer can be of assistance in the choice of an acting company, and through his playreaders he can indicate the sources to be tapped for new plays.

Should the producer have an option on a play that he would like to do but cannot produce at the moment because of casting difficulties or other problems, he could allow the managing director to present the new play in city X. It is understood, of course, that the managing director is not obligated to do the play unless he falls in love with it. For the theatre in city X to be truly wonderful, the managing director must be free to make his own decisions.

If it is feasible, the producer could allow the managing director to use his office (since most producers keep a regular office the year round); if not, the managing director can use the offices of the policy maker of this project. Obviously if the producer gives the managing director some of his office space, he will be contributing to the success of the plan.

Through his advice the producer will give the theatre in city X the benefit of years of theatrical experience. Through his willingness to be the advisory director from afar (and near, of course, whenever possible), he will be giving the theatre in city X the advantages of his prestige and knowledge. And through his desire to allow a script he has under option to be presented he will bring new plays to the world—which is the most any theatre person can contribute.

There is an old saying: "Give to the world the best you have, and the best will come back to you." Strangely enough, without intention of exploitation, the producer may see, through the production of a new script in city X, the possibilities of presenting it on Broadway more quickly than he would have otherwise.

Personally I detest the term "tryout." Plays should not be tried out in one town to see if they will be acceptable in another; this is never a healthy or sound theatre attitude. A play should be done because it is good and can be done well. If successful production of a play in city X stimulates production of the play in other places, then this will be a healthy and progressive spreading of good theatre.

Should it occur that the producer does not have any plays he wants to see done in city X, and the managing director has not found any other manuscripts he likes, there is always a source for a new script: the mother theatre of this plan, Theatre '50, which has had, has and will have five new plays under option every season. I will gladly extend permission (with the authorization of the playwright, of course) to any or all of the twenty theatres to do any of the plays I have under option. The theatres will naturally pay the author 5% of the gross, as specified in the contract.

The intricacies involved in the option of a play (as drawn up by the Dramatists' Guild) are right and fair. A theatre itself cannot take an option because as an organization it does not sign the Minimum Basic Agreement. A producer must take the option and then give the theatre permission to present the play. Within thirty days after the opening of the play, the person who holds the option can pick it up for a "first-class production." Otherwise it reverts to the author. The contract must also provide that the play may be done in repertory during that particular season even if the option is dropped. We have always had the co-operation of playwrights and the Dramatists' Guild in working out these contracts.

What could happen is that in twenty cities in America five new plays would be presented each season—a total of one hundred plays every year. This would be an amazing accomplishment! Should some of the manuscripts be produced at several theatres, and, say, fifty new plays were done every season, it would still be quite an achievement. If ten of the theatres produced the same new play for a three-week run, the playwright's income would be equivalent to 5% of the gross of a thirty-week run, which might make it possible for him to continue writing.

I believe that each one of these theatres should have a resident playwright, so that at least one writer gains a deeper knowledge of the theatre each season at each one of the theatres. A great deal has already been said in this book about the necessity of developing playwriting talent, but I want to add a comment of Thornton Wilder's in reference to a resident playwright at a professional theatre: "What better school for acquiring that dramatist know-how than to hover by a director's elbow while he stages play after play!"

This is the plan of my future. I shall no longer be impatient. I will just roll my sleeves up and get to work. I have never yet rolled my sleeves up without getting the co-operation of theatre people and civic leaders everywhere. I have faith and confidence that a project like this one will merit their co-operation.

Dreams? When a locomotive engine was first invented, was the complicated network of railroads in America envisioned? I believe it was—by some dreamer who was not content with dreams alone. I feel that the establishment of theatres throughout the country is also a dream, but a dream close to reality. If our industries and our sciences can develop, so can our arts.

It means that a great deal of energy should be mustered up to accomplish something beautiful. This energy should certainly be available for positive action. And it should be available not only in the young. It is easier to have ideals when you are nineteen, but if you have them fifteen years later or thirty years later, they are most valuable because with them is the wisdom of experience. Most great leaders in governmental and military affairs are in their sixties and seventies; their knowledge increases their strength as they grow older. But in certain fields age seems to defeat people. It should not be that way in the theatre, for we must combine the wisdom of age with the enthusiasm of youth.

My dream for the future is a theatre which is a part of everybody's life, just as the railroad and the airplane are, a theatre in every town providing entertainment and enlightenment for the audience and a decent livelihood along with high artistic ideals for the theatre worker. This is the goal towards which we must now strive, for which all of us who love the theatre must give our energy, our ideals, our enthusiasm. We can, if we will, create a golden age of the American theatre.

Casts of Productions at Theatre '50

First Season: June to August, 1947.

Staff

Managing Director	Margo Jones
Business Manager	Manning Gurian
Public Relations	Mabel Duke, Watson Associates
Technical Director	A. Joseph Londin
Technical Assistant	Marilyn Putnam
Production & Stage Manager	Joanna Albus
Production Assistants	Jonathan Seymour
	Frank Amy
	Clinton Anderson
	Jack Warden
Treasurer	C. H. Larson

FARTHER OFF FROM HEAVEN
by William Inge

Cast

Sonny Campbell	Martin David
Sarah Campbell	Carol Goodner

Irene Campbell	Rebecca Hargis
Andrew Campbell	Wilson Brooks
Lola Delaney	Betty Greene Little
Ed Delaney	Raymond Van Sickle
Harry Richardson	Frank Amy

HOW NOW, HECATE

by Martin Coleman

Cast

A. B. Murdock	Geoffrey Lumb
Turner	Raymond Van Sickle
Helen Manning	Carol Goodner
Miss Ogilvie	Marga Ann Deighton
Mrs. Trelawney	Betty Greene Little

HEDDA GABLER

by Henrik Ibsen

Cast

Miss Juliana Tesman	Betty Greene Little
Bertha	Marga Ann Deighton
George Tesman	Wilson Brooks
Hedda	Carol Goodner
Mrs. Elvsted	Katharine Balfour
Judge Brack	Geoffrey Lumb
Eilert Lovborg	Tod Andrews

SUMMER AND SMOKE

by Tennessee Williams

Cast

Alma, as a child	Rebecca Hargis
John, as a child	Martin David
The Reverend Winemiller	Raymond Van Sickle
Mrs. Winemiller	Marga Ann Deighton
Dr. John Buchanan, Jr.	Tod Andrews
Alma Winemiller	Katharine Balfour
Jessie Serio	Marilyn Putnam
Nellie Ewell	Pat Papert
Roger Doremus	Clinton Anderson
Dr. John Buchanan, Sr.	Geoffrey Lumb
Mrs. Bassett	Betty Greene Little
Rosemary	Ann Stephens
Vernon	Frank Amy
A Waiter	Jack Warden
Mr. Serio	Wilson Brooks
Archie Kramer	Jonathan Seymour

THIRD COUSIN

by Vera Mathews

Cast

Rosemary Jones	Marilyn Putnam
Pauline Longstreet	Katharine Balfour
Alvin Butterworth	Wilson Brooks
Clifford Perkins	Jack Warden
Carrie Butterworth	Betty Greene Little

Dr. Cutler	Raymond Van Sickle
Harold J. Kirby	Geoffrey Lumb
Bill Avery	Tod Andrews
Mrs. O'Bannon	Marga Ann Deighton

Second Season:
November, 1947 to March, 1948.

Staff

Managing Director	Margo Jones
Business Manager	Manning Gurian
Company Manager	J. B. Tad Adoue, III
Public Relations	Mabel Duke, Watson Associates
Production Designer	Jed Mace
Technical Director	Marshall Yokelson
Technical Assistant	Marilyn Putnam
Production & Stage Manager	Jonathan Seymour
Production Assistants	Clinton Anderson
	Jack Warden
	Charles Taliaferro
	Louise Latham
Treasurer	Billie Baker

THE MASTER BUILDER
by Henrik Ibsen

Cast

Knut Brovik	Vaughan Glaser
Ragnar Brovik	Tod Andrews

Kaia Fosli	Rebecca Hargis
Halvard Solness	Wilson Brooks
Aline Solness	Mary Finney
Doctor Herdal	George Mitchell
Hilda Wangel	Frances Waller

THREE SHORT PLAYS

by Tennessee Williams

Casts

The Last of My Solid Gold Watches

Mr. Charlie Colton	Vaughan Glaser
Porter	Will Bryant
Bob Harper	Tod Andrews

This Property Is Condemned

Willie	Rebecca Hargis
Tom	Charles Taliaferro

Portrait of a Madonna

Miss Lucretia Collins	Katherine Squire
The Porter	Clinton Anderson
The Elevator Boy	Jack Warden
The Doctor	George Mitchell
The Nurse	Mary Finney
Mr. Abrams	Wilson Brooks

THRONG O'SCARLET
by Vivian Connell

Cast

Susie	Rebecca Hargis
Harry Boyle, M.F.H.	Wilson Brooks
Doris Boyle	Mary Finney
Sean Hogan	George Mitchell
Mikey	Jack Warden
Kate	Frances Waller
Hector Maugham	Clinton Anderson
Cynthia Maugham	Katherine Squire
Dolly Brown	Louise Latham
Clark Brown	Tod Andrews
Thaddeus O'Brien	Vaughan Glaser
The Coy One	Carol Jean Rosaire
Sergeant Byrne	Marshall Yokelson
Robinson	Jonathan Seymour
Mrs. Robinson	Gloria Folland

THE TAMING OF THE SHREW
by William Shakespeare

Cast

Baptista	Benedict MacQuarrie
Vincentio	Vaughan Glaser
Lucentio	Jonathan Seymour
Petruchio	Tod Andrews
Gremio	Wilson Brooks

Hortensio	Clinton Anderson
Tranio	George Mitchell
Biondello	Marshall Yokelson
Grumio	Jack Warden
Curtis	Charles Taliaferro
A Pedant	Charley Braswell
Katharine	Katherine Squire
Bianca	Frances Waller
A Servant	Louise Latham
Widow	Mary Finney
Haberdasher	Tommy Woodward
Gregory	Bill Hayter
Philip	Boyd Hill
Officer	Tommy Woodward

(Stage Manager for this production
Rebecca Hargis)

LEMPLE'S OLD MAN
by Manning Gurian

Cast

Dominic	Jack Warden
Hilda	Mary Finney
Pete	Arthur Hill
Tommy	Martin David
Dugan	Clinton Anderson
Clara Harrington	Katherine Squire
Berger	Wilson Brooks
Louise	Louise Latham

Lemple	George Mitchell
Richard Lemple	Tod Andrews
Barbara Adams	Frances Waller
Bill	Charles Taliaferro

THE IMPORTANCE OF BEING EARNEST

by Oscar Wilde

Cast

Lane	Jack Warden
Algernon Moncrieff	Tod Andrews
John Worthing, J.P.	Wilson Brooks
Lady Bracknell	Mary Finney
Hon. Gwendolen Fairfax	Louise Latham
Miss Prism	Katherine Squire
Cecily Cardew	Frances Waller
Rev. Canon Chasuble, D.D.	George Mitchell
Merriman	Clinton Anderson

LEAF AND BOUGH

by Joseph Hayes

Cast

Myra Warren	Mary Finney
Bert Warren	George Mitchell
Aunt Attie	Katherine Squire
Grandpa Nelson	Benedict MacQuarrie

Nan Warren	Frances Waller
Laura Campbell	Betty Greene Little
Frederick Campbell	Wilson Brooks
Glenn Campbell	Jack Warden
Mark Campbell	Tod Andrews

BLACK JOHN

by Barton MacLane

Cast

One-Eye John	Jonathan Seymour
One-Arm John	Marshall Yokelson
The Klootch	Katherine Squire
Rose Larelle	Frances Waller
Honest John	Boyd Hill
Lyme Cushing	Jack Warden
George Cornwallis	Wilson Brooks
Black John	Clinton Anderson
The Simpson Brothers	Jerry Talley
	Charley Braswell
Bandit	Charles Taliaferro
Harry	Bob Kendrick
Corporal Downey	Tod Andrews
The Marshal	George Mitchell
Deputy	Paul Manning
Goldie	Mary Finney
Catteraugas Smith	Benedict MacQuarrie
Benedict Hale	Tad Adoue
Red John	Frank Tennant

Third Season:
November, 1948 to June, 1949.

Staff

Managing Director	Margo Jones
Business Manager	Manning Gurian
Production Designer	Jed Mace
Technical Director	Richard Bernstein
Production and Stage Manager	Jonathan Seymour
Company Manager	J. B. Tad Adoue III
Public Relations	Mabel Duke, Watson Associates
Technical Assistant	Marilyn Putnam
Production Assistants	Rebecca Hargis
	Charles Braswell
Treasurer	Billie Baker

THE LEARNED LADIES
by Molière

Cast

Armande	Romola Robb
Henriette	Frances Waller
Clitandre	John Hudson
Belise	Rebecca Hargis
Ariste	Edwin Whitner
Chrysale	Harold Webster
Martine	Marilyn Putnam
Philaminte	Mary Finney
Trissotin	Jack Warden

Lepine	Tom Ruisinger
Vadius	Clinton Anderson
A Notary	Charles Braswell

HERE'S TO US!

by Shirland Quin

Cast

Mr. McAllistair	Harold Webster
Howard Todd	Edwin Whitner
Kit Tremaine	Mary Finney
Phillipa	Frances Waller
Francis Drinkwater	John Hudson
Charles Crouse	Clinton Anderson
A Stranger	Jack Warden

TWELFTH NIGHT

by William Shakespeare

Cast

Feste	Bill Bray
Curio	George King
Orsino	Jonathan Seymour
Valentine	David Healy
Viola	Frances Waller
Sea Captain	James Maeberry
First Sailor	Bob Hartson
Second Sailor	Jack Boisseau
Sir Toby Belch	Jack Warden
Maria	Mary Finney

Sir Andrew Aguecheek	Edwin Whitner
Olivia	Romola Robb
Malvolio	Clinton Anderson
Antonio	Charles Braswell
Sebastian	John Hudson
Fabian	Tom Ruisinger
First Officer	Jack Boisseau
Second Officer	Bob Hartson
Priest	Harold Webster

SKAAL

by Vivian Johannes

Cast

Old Tink	Edwin Whitner
Ragna	Mary Finney
Selma	Romola Robb
Stefan	John Hudson
Father Thor	Harold Webster
Young Thor	Clinton Anderson
Hilde	Frances Waller
Frithjof	Jack Warden

STING IN THE TAIL

by Tom Purefoy

Cast

Mrs. Stone	Marilyn Putnam
Joseph Bently	Jack Warden
Bridget	Frances Waller

Emily Bently	Rebecca Hargis
Louisa Hackett	Mary Finney
Norah Despard	Romola Robb
Dr. Bianconi	Edwin Whitner
Mr. Turtle	Clinton Anderson

THE SEA GULL
by Anton Chekhov

(Translated by Stark Young)

Cast

Semyon Medvedenko	Charles Braswell
Masha	Rebecca Hargis
Peter Sorin	Harold Webster
Constantine Trepleff	John Hudson
Yacov	Jack Warden
Nina Zaryechny	Frances Waller
Pauline Andreyevna	Romola Robb
Eugene Dorn	Wilson Brooks
Ilya Shamreyeff	Clinton Anderson
Irina Arcadina	Mary Finney
Boris Trigorin	Edwin Whitner

SHE STOOPS TO CONQUER
by Oliver Goldsmith

Cast

Mrs. Hardcastle	Mary Finney
Mr. Hardcastle	Edwin Whitner

Tony Lumpkin	Jack Warden
Kate Hardcastle	Frances Waller
Constance Neville	Romola Robb
First Fellow	Jack Boisseau
Second Fellow	Bob Hartson
Landlord	Charles Braswell
Young Charles Marlow	John Hudson
George Hastings	Wilson Brooks
Diggory	Clinton Anderson
Roger	Tom Ruisinger
Thomas	Bill Adair
Maid	Rebecca Hargis
Sir Charles Marlow	Harold Webster

THE COAST OF ILLYRIA

by Dorothy Parker and Ross Evans

Cast

Mary Lamb	Romola Robb
Charles Lamb	Wilson Brooks
Becky	Margaret McDonald
Emma Isola	Rebecca Hargis
Coleridge	Edwin Whitner
Fanny Kelly	Frances Waller
George Dyer	Harold Webster
Mrs. Kelly	Mary Finney
William Hazlitt	Clinton Anderson
Thomas DeQuincey	John Hudson
Mrs. Crittenden	Edythe Chan
Mr. Crittenden	Jack Warden

Fourth Season:
November, 1949 to June, 1950.

Staff

Managing Director	Margo Jones
Business Manager	Tad Adoue
Assistant Director & Stage Manager	Jonathan Seymour
Lighting Designer	Marshall Yokelson
Costume Designer	Dhu Wray
Public Relations	Mabel Duke, Watson Associates
Production Assistants	Charles Braswell
	Robert Scott
	Margaret O'Neill
	Larry Hageman
	Charles Proctor
Box Office Treasurer	Mary McGrath
General Representative	Manning Gurian

HEARTBREAK HOUSE
by George Bernard Shaw

Cast

Ellie Dunn	Peggy McCay
Nurse Guiness	Loia Cheaney
Captain Shotover	Ben Yafee
Lady Utterword	Virginia Robinson
Hesione Hushabye	Mary Finney
Mazzini Dunn	John Denney

Hector Hushabye	Edwin Whitner
Boss Mangan	Joe Sullivan
Randall Utterword	Gregg Juarez
Burglar	Louis Veda Quince

AN OLD BEAT-UP WOMAN

by Sari Scott

Cast

Utah	Virginia Robinson
Pete	John Denney
Joe Neal	Joe Sullivan

ROMEO AND JULIET

by William Shakespeare

Directed by Jonathan Seymour

Cast

Sampson	Glenn Reid
Gregory	David Healy
Abraham	Stanley Runkel
Balthasar	Donald Howell
Benvolio	Daniel Love
Tybalt	Charles Braswell
Capulet	Louis Veda Quince
Lady Capulet	Virginia Robinson
Montague	Joe Sullivan
Lady Montague	Margaret O'Neill

Prince Escalus	Ben Yafee
Paris	Robert Scott
Romeo	Charles Proctor
Peter	Bill Bray
Nurse	Mary Finney
Mercutio	John Denney
Page to Paris	Martin David
Juliet	Peggy McCay
Friar Laurence	Edwin Whitner
Apothecary	Stanley Runkel
Friar John	James Ray

MY GRANNY VAN

by Loren Disney and George Sessions Perry

Cast

Laura Perry	Margaret O'Neill
Andrew Perry	Joe Sullivan
Granny Van	Mary Finney
Miss Stephanie	Virginia Robinson
George Sessions Perry, Age 8	Randy Lewis
Kate	Jewell Kelly
Uncle Harry	Charles Braswell
Edith Longstreet Clampett	Peggy McKay
Grandfather Van de Venter	Louis Veda Quince
Mr. Thwaites	Edwin Whitner
Dr. Sessions	Ben Yafee
Western Union Boy	Larry Hageman
Constable Critt MacCracken	John Denney

COCK-A-DOODLE DANDY

by Sean O'Casey

Directed by Margo Jones and Jonathan Seymour

Cast

The Cock	Bill Bray
Michael Marthraun	Louis Veda Quince
Sailor Mahan	Ben Yafee
Lorna	Mary Finney
Loreleen	Margaret O'Neill
Marion	Peggy McCay
Shanaar	Edwin Whitner
First Rough Fellow	Charles Braswell
Second Rough Fellow	Larry Hageman
Father Domineer	Richard McCook
The Sergeant	Joe Sullivan
Jack	Bob Cotten
Julia	Virginia Robinson
One-Eyed Larry	Don Howell
The Messenger	John Denney
A Porter	Phil Slater

GHOSTS

by Henrik Ibsen

Cast

Regina Engstrand	Peggy McCay
Engstrand	Ben Yafee

Manders	Edwin Whitner
Mrs. Alving	Mary Finney
Oswald Alving	John Denney

THE GOLDEN PORCUPINE

by Muriel Roy Bolton

Cast

King Louis XI	Louis Veda Quince
Oliver LeDaim	Edwin Whitner
Duchess of Orleans	Mary Finney
Anne of France	Virginia Robinson
Louis of Orleans	John Denney
Charles VIII	Charles Proctor
Count Dunois	Joe Sullivan
Georges D'Amboise	Ben Yafee
Gournay	Charles Braswell
Ann of Brittany	Peggy McCay
Guard	David Healy
Lady-in-Waiting	Margaret O'Neill

SOUTHERN EXPOSURE

by Owen Crump

Cast

Miss Penelope Mayweather	Betty Greene Little
Australia	Jewel Kelly
Carol Randall	Peggy McCay
Mary Belle Tucker	Mary Finney

Avery Randall	Louis Veda Quince
John Salgoud	Charles Braswell
Emmeline Randall	Virginia Robinson
Benjamin Carter	Joe Sullivan

Tourists John Denney, Jonathan Seymour, Edwin Whitner, Ben Yafee, Robert Scott, Charles Proctor, Gloria Gunshor, Barbara Burnett, Mimi Key, Dorothy Lincoln, Dorothy Messick, Lillian Prather, Dee Sparks, Eleanor Speers, Jean Washburn, Mrs. Claud C. Westerfeld.

The Repertory System

First Season

First Week: *Farther Off From Heaven*
Second Week: *How Now, Hecate*
Third Week: The first two plays in repertory
Fourth Week: *Hedda Gabler*
Fifth Week: The three plays in repertory
Sixth Week: *Summer and Smoke*
Seventh Week: *Hedda Gabler* and *Summer and Smoke*
(Split week each)
Eighth Week: *Third Cousin*
Ninth and Tenth Weeks: All five plays in repertory.

Second Season

Each play ran two weeks and the last four weeks of the season were devoted to repertory distributed in the following way:

First Week: *The Taming of the Shrew*
Second Week: *The Importance of Being Earnest*
Third Week: *Throng O'Scarlet* and *Leaf and Bough*
(Split week each)
Fourth Week: The above four plays in repertory.

Third Season

Each play ran three weeks and the last six weeks of the season were devoted to repertory distributed in the following way:

First Week: *The Learned Ladies*
Second Week: *Twelfth Night*
Third Week: *The Importance of Being Earnest* (from the preceding season)
Fourth Week: *The Coast of Illyria* and *Sting in the Tail* (Split week each)
Fifth and Sixth Weeks: All the above plus *She Stoops to Conquer* in repertory.

Fourth Season

The same plan as in the third season, with the last six weeks as follows:

First Week: *Southern Exposure*
Second Week: *Romeo and Juliet*
Third Week: *My Granny Van*
Fourth Week: *Heartbreak House* and *The Golden Porcupine* (Split week each)
Fifth and Sixth Weeks: The above plays in repertory.

A Tentative List of Theatres-in-the-Round

Theatres-in-the-round are springing up so rapidly that it is virtually impossible to present a complete and up-to-date list of them. Many groups have produced a few plays in this medium, but do not use it consistently; I am including a list of all of those about whose activities I was able to obtain some information. Whatever omissions occur in this listing are due to the fact that data was not available on any theatres or groups besides the following:

Permanent Professional Theatres

Arena, New York City
Arena Stage, Washington, D.C.
Penthouse Theatre, Atlanta, Georgia
Penthouse Theatre, Jacksonville, Florida
Playhouse Theatre, Houston, Texas
(Under construction, to open early in 1951)
Ring Theatre, Cleveland, Ohio
Theatre '51, Dallas, Texas

Professional Summer Theatres

Music Circus, Lambertville, New Jersey
(A branch of this theatre is a music circus which functions during the winter in Miami; other music circuses have been established in Hyannis and Danbury and still more are being planned for the summer of 1951.)
Orangeburg, New York
Ringside Theatre, Sea Girt, New Jersey
Salisbury Players, New Hampshire

Other Summer Theatres Which Have Produced Plays in the Round

Hill Barn Summer Theatre, San Mateo, California
Linden Circle Players, Cedar Lake, Wisconsin
Little Theatre of the Downtown YMCA, St. Louis
Milwaukee Players (in the Hayloft Theatre)
Western Springs Theatre, Illinois
A Milwaukee community theatre group which operates in Rhinelander, Wisconsin, during the summer.

Community, College and Semi-Professional Theatres Which Use This Medium Regularly

Alley Theatre, Houston, Texas
Blue Room Players of the Portland Civic Theatre, Oregon
Bowling Green State University, Ohio
Charles Wilhelm's Penthouse Theatre, Altadena, California
Circle Players, Hollywood
Circle Theatre, New York City
Denison University, Granville, Ohio

Dock Street Theatre (in the Green Room), Charleston, S.C.
Fordham University
Gilpin Players, Cleveland
Glendale Centre Theatre, California
Juniata College, Huntingdon, Pennsylvania
Living Room Players of Richmond, Virginia
Old Point Comfort, Virginia (in a hotel room)
Pennsylvania State College (Centre Stage)
Playbox, Pasadena, California
Tufts College Arena Theatre
University of California at Los Angeles
University of Miami (Ring Theatre)
University of Mississippi
University of Texas (Theatre-in-the-Round)
University of Washington (Penthouse Theatre)
University of Wisconsin (Play Circle)
Wayne University Theatre, Detroit
Yakima Valley Junior College, Washington

Community and College Theatres Which Have Used the Medium Occasionally

Alameda Little Theatre, California
Durham Theatre Guild, North Carolina
Erie Playhouse
Alfred Gilliam's group in Tyler, Texas
Good Hope Players, Berkeley, California
John McNeese Junior College, Lake Charles, Louisiana
Masque and Wig Theatre of Lon Morris College, Jacksonville, Texas
Oklahoma College for Women, Chickasha, Oklahoma

Pottsville Undergraduate Center, Pennsylvania
Stadium Theatre, Ohio State University
State College, Pullman, Washington
University of Detroit's Players
Whitman College, Walla Walla, Washington

There are also groups in Beaumont, Texas, and in New Orleans, about which I could obtain no further information.

Selected List of Books and Articles on Theatre-in-the-Round and Related Subjects

No attempt has been made to collect a comprehensive bibliography on the subject; numerous articles have been written about Theatre '50 as well as about arena staging in general. I have selected those which I feel would be of special interest and value to anyone studying the field or starting a theatre of his own.

The only book written on the subject to date is Glenn Hughes's *The Penthouse Theatre.* New York, Samuel French, 1942.

The following books, although not primarily concerned with theatre-in-the-round, contain information and references to either the historical background, experiments in the modern theatre, or the state of the theatre in America today:

Baker, George Pierce. *The Development of Shakespeare as a Dramatist.* New York, Macmillan, 1907.

Bentley, Eric. *The Playwright as Thinker.* New York, Reynal & Hitchcock, 1946.

Cheney, Sheldon. *The Theatre*. New York, Tudor Publishing Co., 1929.

Clurman, Harold. *The Fervent Years*. New York, Knopf, 1945.

Deutsch, Helen, and Hanan, Stella. *The Provincetown*. New York, Farrar, 1931.

Flanagan, Hallie. *Arena*. New York, Duell, Sloan and Pearce, 1940.

———. *Dynamo*. New York, Duell, Sloan and Pearce, 1943.

———. *Shifting Scenes of the Modern European Theatre*. New York, Coward-McCann, 1928.

Freedley, George, and Reeves, John A. *A History of the Theatre*. New York, Crown, 1941.

Gassner, John. *Masters of the Drama*. New York, Random House, 1940.

Hopkins, Arthur. *Reference Point*. New York, Samuel French, 1948.

Houghton, Norris. *Advance from Broadway*. New York, Harcourt, Brace and Co., 1941.

———. *Moscow Rehearsals*. New York, Harcourt, Brace and Co., 1936.

Isaacs, Edith J. R. *Architecture for the New Theatre*. New York, Theatre Arts Inc., 1935.

Jones, Robert Edmond. *The Dramatic Imagination*. New York, Duell, Sloan and Pearce, 1941.

MacGowan, Kenneth. *Footlights Across America (Towards a National Theatre)*. New York, Harcourt, Brace and Co., 1929.

———. *The Theater of Tomorrow*. New York, Boni and Liveright, 1921.

——— and Jones, Robert Edmond. *Continental Stagecraft*. New York, Harcourt, Brace and Co., 1922.

Mantzius, Karl. *A History of Theatrical Art*. New York, Peter Smith, 1903. 6 vols.

Nicoll, Allardyce. *The Development of the Theatre.* Third Edition. New York, Harcourt, Brace and Co., 1946.

———. *World Drama.* New York, Harcourt, Brace and Co., 1950.

Note: Anyone interested in studying the development of theatre-in-the-round in the United States should also consult an unpublished thesis for a Master of Arts degree at Tufts College: J. Burian's "Central Staging: New Force in the Theater."

The reaction of the critics to diverse plays presented in theatre-in-the-round in Dallas are available in the reviews by John Rosenfield in *The Dallas Morning News,* by Clay Bailey and Virgil Miers in *The Daily Times Herald, Dallas,* and in John William Rogers's column "Views and Previews" in the latter newspaper.

In addition to these, numerous articles have been written about arena staging, decentralization of the theatre and specifically about Theatre '50. The list that follows does not attempt to be all inclusive, but I believe it is at least representative of the outstanding comments that have been made in the last few years on the subject.

Adams, J. Donald. "Speaking of Books," *New York Times Book Review,* February 6, 1949.

"Arena Round the Country," *Theatre Arts,* March, 1949.

Atkinson, Brooks. "At the Theater," *New York Times,* April 13, 1949.

———. "Arena Theatre," *New York Times,* May 1, 1949.

———. "Arena Theatre," *New York Times,* June 11, 1950.

———. "Charles Gilpin Players Dedicate their New Playhouse in Cleveland," *New York Times*, December 13, 1949.

———. "They Know What They Want," *New York Times*, May 8, 1949.

Balch, Marston. "Intimacy Is Good Theatre," *Players Magazine*, February, 1949.

Bel Geddes, Norman. "Design for a New Kind of Theatre," *New York Times*, November 30, 1947.

Brown, John Mason. "Seeing Things—in the Round," *Saturday Review of Literature*, April 3, 1948.

Campbell, C. Lawton. "ANTA Presents a Solid Front for the Theatre," *ANTA Magazine*, New York, Spring, 1948.

Cheney, Sheldon. "Hermann Rosse's Stage Designs," *Theatre Arts*, April, 1921.

Cole, Wendell. "Flexible Staging," *Players Magazine*, February, 1949.

Eaton, Walter Prichard. "Why Decentralize?", *New York Times*, December 26, 1948.

Felton, Norman. "Arena Theater—Method for Producing a Play," *National Theatre Conference Bulletin*, April, 1944.

Franklin, Rebecca. "The Newest Theatre Is the Oldest," *New York Times Magazine*, June 11, 1950.

Freedley, George. "Big Business off Broadway," *Saturday Review of Literature*, April 10, 1948.

———. "Central Staging," *Theatre Arts*, March, 1949.

———. "The Stage Today," *The Morning Telegraph* (New York), June 6, 1947.

Freedley, Vinton. "Broadway to Dallas," *Theatre Arts*, March, 1949.

Freud, Ralph. "Central Staging Is Really Old Stuff," *Players Magazine*, December, 1948.

Gilder, Rosamond. "American National Theatre and Academy," *Theatre Arts,* September, 1946.

Green, Harriet. "Gilmor Brown's Playbox," *Theatre Arts,* July, 1935.

Hopkins, Arthur. "The Day of Liberation," *New York Times,* January 9, 1949.

Jones, Margo. "Doing What Comes Naturally," *Theatre Arts,* June, 1949.

———. "A Report on Theatre '48," *ANTA Magazine,* New York, September, 1948.

———. "Theatre '45," *New York Times,* July 15, 1945.

———. "Theatre in the Round," *Players Magazine,* December, 1948.

Jones, Paul. "Backstage," *Atlanta Constitution,* September 18, 1949.

———. "Playhouse in the Sky," *New York Times,* March 12, 1950.

Koch, Jr., Fred. "Arena Formula in Miami," *Players Magazine,* January, 1949.

"Lambertville's Musical Circus," *Cue,* July 6, 1949.

MacGowan, Kenneth. "The Centre of the Stage," *Theatre Arts,* April, 1921.

———. "Virtues of Theatre in the Round," *New York Times,* March 21, 1948.

Martin, Mace. "The Theater of the Year," *Holland's,* October, 1947.

McCleery, Albert. "The Next Step," *Theatre Arts,* March, 1949.

Mitchell, George. "Actor-in-the-Round," *New York Times,* March 28, 1948.

Perry, George Sessions. "Margo Jones Makes Theatrical History," *Cue,* July 10, 1948.

Pinthus, Kurt. "A Plea for More Expressive Acting," *New York Times,* February 1, 1948.

Putnam, Ivan. "So You're Planning an Arena Play," *Junior College Journal,* January, 1948.

Rosenfield, John. "Dallas Theatre '48 Proves a Point," *New York Times,* February 22, 1948.

Rosse, Hermann. "The Circus Theatre," *Theatre Arts,* July, 1923.

Schumach, Murray. "A Texas Tornado Hits Broadway," *New York Times Magazine,* October 17, 1948.

"Theatres of Today and Tomorrow," *Theatre Arts,* July, 1923.

Williams, Tennessee. "A Playwright's Statement on Dallas' Theatre '45 Plans," *Dallas Morning News,* July 22, 1945.

Winkler, A. Eldon. "The Arena Style; a Wartime Style," *Players Magazine,* March, 1943.

Yeaton, Kelly. "Centre Stage," *Players Magazine,* February, 1949.

———. "Directing for Arena Theatre," *Players Magazine,* March, 1949.

———. "How to Start an Arena Theatre," *Players Magazine,* January, 1949.

———. "Look Again, Lanterer!", *National Theatre Conference Bulletin,* March, 1950.

———. "A Pool of Light," *Players Magazine,* April, 1949.

Quotations used in Chapter V are from the following plays:

Chekhov, Anton. *The Sea Gull.* (Translated by Stark Young.) New York, Charles Scribner's Sons, 1939.

Ibsen, Henrik. *Hedda Gabler.* (Translated by William Archer and Edmund Gosse.) New York, Charles Scribner's Sons.

O'Casey, Sean. *Cock-a-Doodle Dandy.* London, Macmillan, 1949.

Shakespeare, William. *The Taming of the Shrew.* (Cambridge Edition Text.)

———. *Twelfth Night.* (Cambridge Edition Text.)

Shaw, George Bernard. *Heartbreak House,* in *Six Plays.* New York, Dodd, Mead and Co., 1948.

Williams, Tennessee. *Summer and Smoke.* New York, New Directions, 1948.

———. *Twenty-Seven Wagons Full of Cotton.* New York, New Directions, 1945.

Index